To "Red" Press
with best wishes,

Gene Marden

DEVILS AMONG ANGELS
A JOURNEY FROM PARADISE AND HELL TO LIFE

BY
SAMUEL MARDER

COVER PHOTO BY
EDVARD LIEBER

EDITED BY
FRAN GOLDSTEIN

DESIGN BY
ROBBIE ROBBINS

ISBN: 978-1-61377-817-3

16 15 14 13   1 2 3 4

DEVILS AMONG ANGELS
A JOURNEY FROM PARADISE AND HELL TO LIFE

A COLLECTION OF SHORT STORIES AND POEMS

BY
SAMUEL
MARDER

Dedication

To the memory of my parents
Berl and Esther Marder

Acknowledgement

There are times when words cannot express all that is in our hearts. Nothing I would write could ever adequately describe the warmth and appreciation that I feel for my dear friends Howard and Debbie Jonas. I am deeply grateful for their interest, encouragement, kindness and willingness to bring these pages to light. May they and their families be blessed with long, healthy lives filled with joy and happiness.

TABLE OF CONTENTS

Part 4: Holocaust Poems

Introduction

By Irving Greenberg

The pain, destruction and loss in the Holocaust was infinite—so we can never have enough survivor accounts to depict every aspect of this endless nightmare. Sam Marder's report—*Devils and Angels: A Journey from Paradise and Hell to Life*—is one of the most unusual accounts I have ever read. It is a unique mixture of fiction, autobiography and poetry. The fiction—often articulated in a kind of magical realism style—describes the world that Sam (and all of us) lost in the Shoah. The fragments of autobiography that follow are heartbreaking, yet written with great restraint. He tells of a devoted father who kept people's spirits up; even when deeply sick, he willed to go on for the sake of his family. Yet he was finally felled by typhoid and hunger, leaving Sam with memories and lost love that haunt him to this day. We learn of Herr Schwartz, the good German, who tried in vain to save the family by hiding them but could not convince them to try. We encounter Professor Nowack, a shy, agitated, anti-Semitic, self-destructive concert violinist. With surprising generosity of spirit, he restored Sam's calling as a violinist after the war ended, by giving him personal recognition of his talent. He gave the young survivor free lessons, since his family could not afford the training given their status as refugees in a Displaced Persons Camp. Later, the family tried to return the favor—

only to discover that Nowack had betrayed to the Nazis a Jewish friend who helped him in his studies. Sam tells of life and suffering under the Nazis and of the differing form of hell under the Communists. He tells of survival, of persistence after death, of loving kindness coming after devastatingly horrifying experiences. The final section gives us the poems—of longing for God, of haunting memories of father, of painfully learned harsh lessons about human nature, of powerfully preserved faith that defied the experience and of hope that transcended the horrors. Each survivor's account is a "brand snatched from the fire" (Zechariah 3:2)—a eulogy for a lost world and family, written with heart's blood. In Sam Marder's account, it all adds up to beautiful music—a symphony dedicated to life and hope and a triumph of human spirit over the worst that can be done to it. I don't know where Sam Marder got the strength to go on, to still believe, to make beautiful music. I am all the more grateful to him for this account. Every reader will be challenged to do no less to affirm life, to turn suffering into a spur to better living. We honor God and our martyrs by remembering and treasuring the memory. This book does that noble work for us.

Rabbi Irving (Yitzchak) Greenberg, is President Emeritus of CLAL, the National Jewish Center of Jewish Learning, and is author of many articles and books, among them: A Cloud of Smoke, Pillar of Fire, Voluntary Covenant, Living in the Image of God, Judaism and Christianity, For the Sake of Heaven and Earth, Conventional Pluralism.

Foreword

By Alan J. Yuter

Most of Samuel Marder's writing in this book contains material about prewar life in Eastern Europe, some of his Holocaust experiences, and his concern about the post Holocaust world. I have chosen one poem and one short story as a basis for my comments in this Foreword.

In order to get to know the author, I suggest you read first the poetry at the end of the book. His poetry makes a statement, as it soars in its simplicity, to a dimension so sacred that it cannot be contained in the language capsule that is by convention called "prose."

In the poem *Shoah*, meaning "Holocaust," Marder writes:
"Bodies drift in deadly silence
On a bloodied river Prut,
Faces waxen, eyes glazed,
Staring at a sky in mourning
Wrapped in ashen gray.
The world had no room for them,
Nor soul enough for them to pray."

The dead remain sort of alive, staring accusingly, as gray colorless reflections enshrouding the unburied—and unwanted— Jewish dead. On the surface, the words, like rivers of blood, run their course. The attentive reader quickly realizes that little humans are cosmic players. After all, it is the sky that is both in mourning and enshrouded "in ashen gray," unburied. In order to appreciate the poetic narrative fully, read slowly, with engagement, and ask, "what is the narrator's soul trying to awaken, as if from the dead, in me, the reader?"

With a lyric prose, Samuel Marder complains to God, out of faith, with pain, because he is human, and with serenity, because he believes that the divine in humankind must defeat the demonic, chaotic and evil forces that infect our world. For Marder, in order to believe, one must see the serenity that is fogged by the hardest questions humans can ask. And herein lies the message, the art, and the soul of the artist.

In his short story "The Noodnik," Marder's confessional narrator is Leibel, meaning "lion," as in "the lion of Judah." Some see Leibel as a noodnik, a bothersome person, a corrective character, a modern, little man with a great mission, a miniature Messiah. Leibel appears small but strives for moral greatness. He can read into the minds of men. After all, prophecy is given to children and fools in our times, so Chelm, the city of fools, becomes one of penetrating prophecy. Leibel informs his reader that when the Messiah comes, he will expect to find noodniks, who will be the first to be invited to the Messiah's table. Chelm is the least of cities and its noodniks are, by dint of their "otherness," uniquely gifted to see and say things as they are.

Moses and Aaron were noodniks. And as prophets, were speakers, seeing and then responding to evil. Like Moses, Abraham the patriarch pestered God to do the right thing by Sodom. What appears at first glance to be a silly soliloquy now appears to the attentive reader to be the mission and message of Marder's mind. On one hand, Leibel is committed to the world construction and religion of the simple Orthodox Jew; on the other hand, Marder's narrator, the proxy for the narrating prophet/poet, is making a clarion call to his readers. The moral status quo is not of our making; inattention to evil is our moral undoing. When simple people talk, their hurts bother us. We can look at and hear their hurts as annoying intrusions on our comfort, or take the Divine perspective, to realize malchut Shaddai, the Messianic Kingdom of God, the malchut shamayim, the Kingdom of Heaven on this pedestrian earth.

By referring to Scripture, we are told that God really listens to noodniks. In other words, those who complain will find in God an attentive, if metaphorical, ear. The narrator's voice is Orthodox, but his world, like Noah's ark, has room for everybody. At the end of the monologue, Leibel the prophetic noodnik complains about his business competitor, speaking ill about him. And in his speaking ill about this fellow, Leibel, the messianic lion of Judah, corrects himself as a precondition for correcting others. The attentive reader realizes that Marder's theme resonates in the Mishnaic tract called Ethics of the Fathers.

Sam Marder has here created an ethical and ecumenical world with simple words that offer a complex challenge. Addressing Christian as well as Jewish readers, Marder's own Orthodox point of view is informed by a post-modern pluralism that makes room for dissent and competitors. And the hurting and aggrieved, whom the comfortable experience as inconvenient and troublesome, are Marder's, concern.

Leibel is both angel and devil. And so are we, the engaged readers. A generation after the Holocaust, Sam Marder is challenging his readers with the Deuteronomic call to "choose life."

The first person narration is a deft device that leads the reader to hear the call to be a noodnik, an angelic agent, a miniature Messiah. We all have the potential for selfishness and greatness.

Like this story, the entire volume is written in a deceptively simple, measured, evocative poetic prose. This Orthodox thinker is artistically engaged, theologically subtle, and probably more "modern" than we would expect. Marder is blessed with a third eye, in the back of his head, looking inward into his own soul, religiously and secularly informed, to write in art, a theology for modernity.

Rabbi Yuter taught at University of Maryland (Baltimore County), and has served as an Adjunct Professor of Hebrew Literature, Baltimore Hebrew University. He taught Bible, Jewish law, and Jewish thought at the joint program of Fairleigh Dickenson University/Institute for Traditional Judaism. S'micha was granted by the Chief Rabbi of Israel, Rabbi Mordecai Eliyahu, Rabbi Moses D. Tendler of Yeshiva University, and Rabbi David Halivni, who granted the Yadin Yadin ordination. Rabbi Yuter holds a Ph.D. in Hebrew Literature from New York University. He now teaches Jewish law at Midreshet Devotah and Machon Pardes in Jerusalem. He is author of The Holocaust in Hebrew Literature.

Preface

Many years ago, friends urged me to write about my family's experiences during the Holocaust and our deportation to Transnistria. But I was hesitant to do so. I preferred to go on with my life—to concentrate on the present and the future—rather than to look back and think about the past.

But I began feeling a sense of responsibility to write after my sister and I visited our hometown of Czernowitz in the early 1990s. As one might imagine, the trip was incredibly emotional for us. We were flooded with memories—both the good times as children before the war and the horrible times that befell us once the war started. On that trip, we befriended a man who wrote about his experiences during the Nazi period. Although we shared similar experiences, our actual stories were quite different. I felt compelled to write, realizing that it was my duty to share my experience with others because the tellers of the stories were dying out. I was reminded of my thoughts as a young child of 10 during our internment in Transnistria. Often, when I was a heartbeat away from death, I would wonder whether anyone of us would be left to tell the world about the hell we were going through.

Once I started writing, I was amazed at how often my mind was sidetracked from the Transnistria experiences. Instead, I found myself writing poems and short stories about my early, pre-war childhood. It took some time for me to be able to revisit my memories of the Nazi years. These stories depict just a fraction of my experiences in Transnistria that reflect the best and worst of humanity.

Both the fiction and non-fiction stories and poems about my life as a child in Romania and family visits to pre-war Poland reflect a world that vanished in front of my eyes. I wanted to share my memories of the vibrant culture and communities that will never again exist. Most of the people who lived in those areas were decimated along with their cemeteries. But I also wanted to bring out the lighter side of that world before the war. So I hope the reader will find some humor in the fictional stories ("Purim in Korolivke," "The Wandering Preacher" and "The Noodnik of Chelm"), as well as in some of the poems.

May the memory of all lost be for a blessing.

I would like to express my deep appreciation to each of the following people for their help with this book's publication: Ted Adams for his utmost cooperation during this book's publication; Fran Goldstein for her invaluable editorial suggestions; David Haas for his kindness and patience with photography; Ed Lieber for lending his unique artistic input; Robbie Robbins for designing the book; and Dr. Carol Weinstein for her patience and help with my computer problems. Lastly and very importantly, I want to thank my wife, Sonia, for her invaluable comments during the writing of the manuscripts.

Samuel Marder,
Riverdale, N.Y.
June 2013

PART 1
WORKS OF FICTION

Itzik the Watchmaker

When Itzik the watchmaker was about to join the heavenly family, there was an uproar in heaven. Angels were standing in the celestial corridors feverishly exchanging the latest rumor about the new arrival. They were anxious to find out who Itzik was because, somehow, it became known that he would be arriving with a request and a bundle of strange complaints.

But, still, was that a good enough reason to generate so much attention in heaven and ignite the angels' imagination? After all, he was not on the select register of the great and famous, nor did his name appear in the huge file of the poor and destitute. There certainly was no mention of him in the gigantic, overloaded list of candidates for Gehenom[1]. Even Satan himself was observed shrugging his shoulders in a who-cares manner when Itzik's name was brought up. That in itself was unusual. Whoever heard of Satan being indifferent to human behavior? Why would Satan, who is known to be prying into every person's life, show so little interest in Itzik's activities? Isn't it true that greed pierces its claws equally, making deep dents in the souls of rich and poor, unknown and famous? What was so special about Itzik and his requests that would leave Satan so disinterested, causing him to show such rare aloofness at the mention of his name? And why would his expected arrival create so much interest and excitement among angels?

The imps in Heaven spared no effort in trying to get some information on Itzik and his earthly activities, probably anxious to prove their usefulness to Satan, their superior. They worked like beavers and were determined to dig up all available facts about this "strange" watchmaker. (Unfortunately, the devil's helpers seem to be more inquisitive than the angels because of their propensity to gossip. It is difficult to understand why, but the desire to find fault often conjures up more energy than the search for good.) As it turned out, there was nothing unusual about Itzik's status in the circles of earthly society. Itzik had not been considered a highly learned man on earth. As a matter of fact, people ignored him and wise men—even some holy men—found him amusing. "Because Itzik's questions and complaints about God's universal order," they said, were "out of sorts and not realistic." They referred to him as Itzik the Dreamer. Although Itzik felt alone and somewhat ostracized, he was adamant; he did not budge.

"I simply want to know why the world was not made to run like a good watch in which all wheels turn in the proper direction. If I, a simple watchmaker, can fix a watch that works with reasonable precision," he said, "the Everlasting Creator of everything that exists on earth and heaven and originator of perfection itself, could have certainly applied, at least, the same precision and high standards of a good watchmaker when He created the world." Unless, of course, Itzik thought, His wish was not to do so. If that was the case, Itzik wanted to know why, "because man's suffering due to his imperfections is heartbreaking."

Itzik had even more questions: If God wants man to behave in certain ways, why create him with volatile character traits that make it difficult for him to follow God's commands?

Itzik remembered having learned that man is being sent to Earth and tested, and that God gave man the choice between good and evil. "But how much choice does man have?" he asked, given his limited self-awareness? Even animals seem to fare better in their world than man does in his environment, Itzik thought.

He knew that people strongly disagreed with his comparison of man to animal. "How could you compare them?" his friends would ask. After all, aren't man's accomplishments self-evident?"

But Itzik was not impressed.

"Do you know of an animal who destroys his own surroundings and poisons the waters his children and grandchildren will have to drink from?" Itzik said. "It all depends what accomplishment means to you. If man knows more about the physical world than about his own nature, I would hardly call it progress. How much has man contributed toward his own happiness?" he asked.

"Dear God," he would say, "Since You chose to create us with incomplete insight into our own nature, You know that we are partly blind to the mistakes we make. Why, then, condemn us for them?"

Itzik also wanted to understand some of God's choices and decisions. He had problems with God's management (or indirect management, as he used to refer to it at times) of the Earth and its inhabitants. "All I am asking for," he said, "is an explanation I can understand."

Having been a deeply religious person, Itzik was consumed by a burning desire to understand God's world and plagued by a stubborn preoccupation with justice. He believed strongly in God but had great misgivings about "the sad state in which God allowed the world to drift since creation, letting it wallow in its problems."

Itzik had trouble understanding why the Creator added sickness to health and evil to good. He was amazed that God exclaimed: "All was good!" What was so good when God knew that man would soon mess it up and turn a Garden of Eden into earthly hell?

"And what about the devil?" Itzik wanted to know. "What did He create him for? Even without Satan's instigation, people manage to treat one another with scorn and hate and kill each other. It is pretty obvious that the devil is really not needed. Quite an impressive number of humans, some of them ready to swear by their holy books that they are God-lovers, are doing Satan's work quite faithfully and competently."

Itzik wanted to know why man was born to eventually die? Once we get a glimpse of life, it's time for us to leave this world.

He knew that the usual answer would be: "The old must make room for the new. That is probably the best possible human answer," he said. "But for God, nothing is impossible! He can have life continue by creating more space in His endless universe.

"From my limited view it doesn't make sense. This entire struggle, for what? Life is a precious gift from God. I wonder how the Everlasting One would view a human who gives a gift and then wants it back? I believe in the resurrection of the dead some day. But, in the meantime, why cause pain and grief through death?

"And what about animals?" Itzik wanted to know. "Someone should speak up on their behalf, too. They don't have it so well, either. What have they done to deserve the kind of lives they live? What sin have they committed to be relegated to an awful way of existence? Why do so many of them have to kill and eat each other alive for their survival? Why didn't the Eternal One with His Supreme wisdom design a more equitable system of sustenance for them,?"

Tormented by these questions, Itzik could not find peace and continued searching for answers.

Although wise men, scholars and even some holy people, would chuckle lightheartedly at his questions, finding them odd, naive and amusing, deep down they knew that Itzik's questions were not really that strange.

Time's clock kept ticking, and as our watchmaker grew older, he never gave up praying and never lost his sensitivity, love and compassion for God's world. Through the years, his list of questions increased by leaps and bounds, as did his complaints. Even though he knew that one is not supposed to question the Eternal's ways, he just couldn't understand why God would create a world that even a simple watchmaker could find fault with.

"Perhaps God has His own ethereal reasons for letting the world go on the way it does," Itzik said, "but, if it is so, why turn it into a mystery for those who are trying to have a better understanding of His work?" Itzik felt that the desire to pray for a satisfactory explanation from a perfect Being possessing eternal wisdom and goodness should not be considered too much.

Itzik sought answers to his many questions, hoping to bring peace to his excruciatingly pained conscience. He first looked into the writings of holy men. However, eventually, he lost faith in the knowledge of mortal experts, even holy ones, to answer his questions about God's workings ways.

"I saw so much affliction and anguish in my lifetime that urgently need explanations, so many problems no mortal seems to be capable of solving and questions no human being can satisfactorily answer," Itzik was overheard saying with a sense of utter pain and frustration. "I have decided not to budge until God himself will grant me a moment from His eternal time to answer these questions that have been nagging me all my life. I am not requesting them just for myself, but for the sake of billions upon billions of his creatures who go through life in utter misery and extreme suffering. There must be answers to my questions, and the only authority to provide an answer is the Creator himself, blessed be He."

Itzik, therefore, embarked on a program of inner purification and special prayer. He made a covenant between himself and his conscience that, come what may, he would not give up. He tried to muster all the stubbornness at his disposition and insist on getting access to the Eternal One, so that these questions torturing his mind and soul would finally come to rest. If this encounter did not occur during his lifetime on Earth, it might, God willing, have to take place when the time arrives for him to join the world of truth in heaven.

His request was expressed with such power, urgency and depth of feeling that, although it had been ignored by his earthly fellow human beings, it drew attention among the angels in the upper spheres. As soon as his request arrived, it was put in a special file. In fairness to the watchmaker, it was decided in heaven that the details of his questions would not be made known until Itzik arrived.

Heaven does not have news leaks. Even the imps, after trying very hard to come up with some news about the watchmaker's requests, did not succeed. All they discovered was that Itzik's appeal was both urgent and unusually daring, and that it had something to do with complaints about the order of the world. Itzik's questions created an atmosphere of agitation and anticipation in heaven. It seems the angels also had questions stashed away in their consciences that weighed heavily on them—questions that nagged them but they never dared to ask.

"Who knows," they whispered secretly to one another with trepidation and anxiousness, "perhaps great and powerful human compassion might bring about a change in God's silence." The angels were hopeful, but Satan laughed the whole idea off. He had a completely blasé attitude about the watchmaker's questions and complaints. Had he seen some possibility of Itzik's requests getting attention in heaven, he would have certainly been upset. However, he was absolutely certain that there was very little to worry about. "Nothing will ever change on Earth," he exclaimed with a mocking smile. He could simply not understand why these "silly, naive" angels were so excited.

Now, when Itzik arrived at the gates of heaven, he immediately asked to see his Heavenly Father. Fortunately, because angels, as one would expect, are goodhearted souls, they didn't break out in laughter at this preposterous request. Instead, they told him patiently and politely that his request, as far as they knew, could not be met, but that they would try their best to relate the message to Michael and Gabriel, the angels nearest to God, and would give Itzik an answer as soon as they received one.

What happened after is difficult to tell, but Itzik could swear by the holy scriptures that the encounter with the Eternal One had finally taken place; and this is how he recounted his experience verbatim:

"I could not see anything, but I felt that I was in the presence of God, so I began speaking to Him as follows:

'Blessed be Thou Creator of the Universe and Father of all that it contains! I have some questions that I must ask You. Please don't blame me for doing so. It is not out of impudence that I stand now before You. Throughout my earthly life, I have tried to make use of all my limited thinking ability, which You had granted me. This I did, not

only for the benefit of my own survival but also out of a strong desire to gain a deeper understanding of Your world and out of compassion for my fellow creatures.'"

Itzik wanted so much to pour out his soul to God, but decided that this opportunity of speaking to the Everlasting One must not be lost. He, therefore, decided to direct his questions with the professional precision of a fine, meticulous watchmaker, one question after another, quickly, to make sure he would not be stopped cold in the middle of his presentation.

After it was over, Itzik felt, perhaps by intuition, that somewhere not far in the distance, God was listening attentively. He looked hard hoping to catch, at least, a glimpse of something visible, but all he could discern was the presence of a gigantic eye-blinding light, unlike anything he had ever seen before, enveloped in an ashy haze through which an entity seemed to have cast a gentle smile at him...

That transcendental experience suddenly created in him a complete transformation. His perceptions, formed throughout his life and his concept of time working with clocks, drastically changed.

Now, in his new state, Itzik came to the realization that finite man cannot expect to comprehend the Infinite—a realm that transcends human intelligence. He was now in a world where questioning and striving for answers dissolves into nothingness.

A sense of peace overtook him. No more was he consumed by a burning desire to understand the Heavenly order. He felt that he was an integral part of that order. He was at peace—perfect, heavenly peace.

Purim in Korolivke

You never heard of Korolivke? I am not surprised. It was a village—or shtetl—nestled in the middle of nowhere, and only the neighboring villages knew it existed. Korolivke was located in an area of Eastern Europe called Galicia, which had once been part of the Austrian-Hungarian Empire. The area, like many others in the region, changed hands almost like shares do on the stock market. It was once part of Poland, was later annexed by the Soviet Union, and is now part of the Ukraine.

Korolivke's population consisted of a majority of Poles and Ukrainians and a minority of Jews (which are the focus of our story). It consisted of several dozen low-lying village huts whose straw roofs seemed larger than the houses they covered. Its narrow dirt roads provided the village with more dust than it could handle, and during rains, with more mud than human feet could manage.

Although the Jewish population was small, Korolivke boasted two synagogues—a rich and a poor one. The poor house of prayer did not own as many holy books as the rich one, but it was blessed for generations with more worshipers. No one knows why, but the poor had a theory: They felt that God loves the poor; that's why he creates more of them.

Whether rich or poor, Korolivke's citizens were proud people. And the poor did not feel any less important than the more well-to-do.

Korolivke's standards for wealth were modest. The only requirement for being considered rich was being able to afford to eat chicken or meat more than once a week, have butter on the bread at the breakfast table, and perhaps own a goat or two, or maybe even a cow.

Korolivke, like the rest of the world, had its share of problems related to "class." Although there was no real middle class, there was a silent understanding that those who refused to consider themselves poor were automatically members of the middle class. They didn't feel like attending the poor synagogue and the rich were not exactly overjoyed when the "not so poor" worshippers whom the town dubbed "di nisht ahin un nisht aher mentshalech," meaning "the not here not there little people," showed up and made themselves comfortable in their prayer house.

Although it was a small town, Korolivke's residents were no less refined than those of larger towns. I should think that if the whole world were to deal with its problems the way Korolivke did, there would be fewer wars and murders.

The reason was quite simple. Korolivke had different ways of dealing with its frustrations than the rest of the world. They fought with words. Even when curses were flying during arguments, you could feel that underneath it all, people cared for one another.

Korolivke also boasted a rabbi and an assistant, a traditional bath, a market, a chimney cleaner, an orphanage, a cemetery and a Heder[1]. It even had its own beggar—a celebrity in his own right. Everyone knew and respected Bunim the Beggar. Who would not respect someone who knows everything about everyone in shtetl?

Korolivke also had an inn where travelers could stay overnight, and where the Ukrainian and Polish peasants from the nearby villages would come in to have a drink.

All year around, the relationship between the peasants and the Jews was as normal as one could expect in that part of world. Some of the peasants had their favorite Jews; they called them by their nicknames and joked around.

---

1 *Religious school; literal translation—room.*

But that was during times of sobriety. On holidays like Christmas and Easter, when the drinking reached higher levels, the peasants became merrier. They entered the shtetl, broke some windows, beat up a few people, and then returned to their homes singing merrily at the top of their voices.

Korolivke had many unique characters, probably the most famous of whom were Yoine and Fishl. Yoine was a sort of ambassador-at-large of the rich synagogue, while Fishl was his equivalent at the poor prayer house. Everyone in Korolivke had a nickname.

Fishl was called the dancer, and with good reason. His walk took on the character of a complicated dance maneuver. He swayed his body right and left like a dancer with every step, and when people asked him "what is that dancing all about? Where is the wedding?" He would ask: "How would you know about weddings? You are so smart you couldn't tell the difference between a wedding and a funeral!"

Yoine's and Fishl's weekly arguments were an integral part of the shtetl. No one dared—nor did they have a chance to—intervene. Their disputes were heated and uncompromising. Whether they liked each other or not, no one knew; but one thing was certain; they needed one another. Every Sabbath, whenever Yoine walked out of the prayer house, his eyes immediately searched for Fishl, who would normally wait for him on the corner of Market Street. Even cold winter days did not stop them from meeting. If, for some reason, they did not meet on a Sabbath, both walked around with long faces and looked as if they had been cheated out of an important part of their lives.

Their meetings usually began with the common Yiddish Sabbath greeting:

"Good Shabbes[2] to you, Reb Fishl; nu? What's new in this little world of ours?"

"What can be new? The world is the same as it was last Shabbes. Remember what it says in the Talmud, "'Nothing is new under the sun.'"

"Who says it's written in the Talmud?"... And soon a new subject for an argument was born.

2 Sabbath.

Fishl was of small build and chubby, and when he walked he looked like a barrel rolling down the street. He spoke with a loud, high-pitched voice and was also called The German, because he was clean-shaven and wore a modern suit—a rarity in Korolivke in those days. The problem with his suit was that its better days were long past and its pockets were filled with holes big enough to let through anything they were entrusted with. Luckily, that did not present a problem for Fishl, since he didn't have a penny to his name. However, the pride of wearing modern clothing with a bowler hat to boot in a prayer house filled with worshippers dressed in Hassidic garb compensated generously for his empty pockets. It proved beyond doubt that he was his own man—an independent soul.

In contrast to Fishl, Yoine was thin and tall. He also had the honor of having two nicknames. The first was Yoine der Koyne, meaning the buyer. He had a special talent for ending up paying more for everything he bought than anyone else in shtetl. Yoine was a trusting person, and all the peasants in the market knew that he would pay any price he was quoted, rather than negotiate. When people would meet him in the market and ask jokingly: "Nu, Yoine, what bargain did you buy today?" Yoine would say: "What would you know about bargains when you are not such a big bargain yourself?"

His second nickname was Yoine the Moyne—the counter, since he was the one appointed to count the contributions made to the orphan house and other town needs. Yoine dressed in traditional Hassidic garb and was soft-spoken; until, that is, Fishl confronted him. Once the two met, Yoine suddenly assumed a new personality and matched Fishl's shouting decibel for decibel. Often it seemed as if each one yelled at himself. The themes covered during such arguments were innumerable. However, the subject matter was not as important as the act of arguing itself. Everyone knew that if Yoine would say, for instance, that Purim[3] was a holiday, Fishl would try to prove him wrong. Neither Fishl nor Yoine were simpletons. They constantly quoted commentators. While, the source of those quotes may have been Ukrainian or Polish sayings, Yoine and Fishl were convinced that they were actually quoting important commentators such as Rashi, Ibn Ezra, the Ramban, Tosefot and

3 Holiday celebrating a foiled plot by Haman, high official to King Ahasuerus of ancient Persia, to kill all the Jews in its Empire.

others. Bystanders were often mesmerized by the length of the discussions and tried to figure out who would win the argument. However, the results of the contests were usually inconclusive and the onlookers left raising their shoulders good-naturedly, wondering what it was all about.

Enough about Fishl and Yoine. Let's resume our story.

Like pious residents of other shtetls, Korolivke's people took their holidays seriously. One of the most festive holidays was Simkhat Torah.[4]

On this holiday, people competed—sometimes beyond their meager means—to buy the honor of chanting the prayer of Atto Horeyso before the opening of the arc. With uninhibited joy and enthusiasm, the worshipers danced and circled the synagogue carrying the Torahs. Children ran around with little flags topped with apples and candles, and if one of the little flag holders overindulged in bragging about his flag, it would mysteriously catch fire...

Yes! Simkhat Torah was a happy holiday in Korolivke. But it was during the holiday of Purim that the shtetl took on a special appearance. The men of the households took to whiskey with religious devotion. Housewives and young girls rushed, as if there was a fire, from house to house with Purim presents in their hands for neighbors and friends, and children frolicked about the town's narrow roads with masks on their faces making noises with rattles late into the evening. No one knew where the brandy and sweets came from, considering that throughout the rest of the year Korolivke wallowed in poverty. Korolivke created its own miracles, especially on holidays. (For example, on Passover the village bakery produced its own unleavened bread and on other holidays they found ways of having enough flour to bake sweets and other delicacies.) How these changes took place will remain a mystery till the end of time.

Each Purim, the Rabbi of Korolivke, Reb Shimshon, disguised himself and entertained the children in the orphanage. One year he showed up dressed as a lion; another year he disguised himself as a cat with a long tail and large whiskers crawling on all fours. The children just loved it!

Even Bunim the Beggar acted differently on Purim. Throughout the year he would go around from house to house with his hand

---

4 *Celebration of having completed the reading of the Torah through the year.*

outstretched for a coin or two. But, "on Purim," he said, "who needs money?" He went from door to door with a glass in his hand asking housewives to refill it with wine or whiskey.

"I am not particular when it comes to drink and sweets," he confided to them with a secretive wink and an intimate smile on his face.. It was a technique carefully rehearsed through the years, which led to remarkable success. He always wound up with all the liquor he needed and pockets filled with Hamentashen.[5]

"Today, I am equal to everybody," he boasted with a proud smile. "I can be just as drunk as Yosl the Rich," and he had a point. Although no one in Korolivke could compare himself to Yosl the Rich, Bunim drank so much on Purim that by the time the town's clock reached midday he could be found lying on the steps of the public bath at the edge of town so groggy that he could not tell whether he was celebrating or mourning.

In short, there was no town merrier on Purim than Korolivke. Everyone was happy.

Everyone except Shmelke, also known as Shmaysl, (a Yiddish nickname meaning The Lasher), a name that had been bestowed on him for lashing himself while serving his customers. (More on his nickname later).

Shmaysl made his living selling eggs, honey, sour pickles and horseradish in front of his house. The aroma of his sour pickles reached as far as the Turkish tower at the end of town. His horseradish was so potent that when it was used at the Passover Seder—as is the tradition—eyes kept watering till the end of the meal, so that everyone in Korolivke sang Chad Gadya[6] with tears in their eyes.

It's not surprising that Shmaysl's horseradish was in heavy demand before Passover. His customers stood in a line that spanned several streets, and the tumult was enough to make you feel that Korolivke was in battle. The pandemonium would get so out of hand that the village policeman, Mikhail, had to be called to keep some semblance of order.

"Panie (Mr.) Mikhail, just take a look how this character with the red scarf is trying to get ahead in line! Hey—Hey—Who does she think she is?"

---

5 Small triangle cakes filled with various fruits.
6 Poem sung at the end of the Passover Seder.

"Well, well! Take a look how Yankl's wife is flattering Mikhail to get herself in front of everybody! Hey, Panie Mikhail, come here! Look how that good-for-nothing just got here and is trying to work her way ahead of us! That's not fair! Panie Mikhail this, Panie Mikhail that."

Finally, when Mikhail felt the women were going to drive him out of his mind, he ran off to the inn for a drink to escape the screaming customers. Actually, it was not a drink; the situation required more than that. After returning with an empty bottle in his hand, it became obvious that its contents had given him enough courage to stand up to the housewives. Sure enough, he blew his whistle and began yelling at the top of his voice until the veins on his neck looked like they were going to burst:

"Quiet, women! Quiet! Quiet, I said! If you don't stop screaming, I'm going to chase everybody away and nobody will have horseradish for Passover." He finished his brief lecture with an energetic spit on the ground to prove that he meant business. Do you think, perhaps, that the women were scared? Housewives of Korolivke don't scare so easily!

Shmaysl's Nickname

Just as Shmaysl had a regular clientele of housewives anxious to buy his tasty food products, he also had other types of eager customers. They included bees, flies and other insects that he justifiably referred to as "flying curses." Their hutzpah[7] was, to say the least, profoundly annoying. They gathered around Shmaysl with no less enthusiasm than the housewives, and attacked his goods with the expertise only bees, flies and insects are capable of. In addition, they seemed to prefer having a taste of him before indulging into his delicacies, so that with his right hand he served his customers, and with his left he kept slapping himself trying to ward off these unwelcome guests; hence, his nickname, Shmaysl (The Lasher).

The men of Krivch used to joke with him:

"Hey, Shmaysl, you don't need to get malkes[8]: You get them all year."

Everyone in Korolivke knew Shmaysl. They always thought of him as an honest and smart man. Their respect for him increased even more after the egg story became well known in all of Korolivke.

---

7 Nerve.
8 Symbolic lashes over the back that observant people give each other before Yom Kippur—the day of forgiveness.

One year, Shmaysl began noticing eggs missing every week from his barn. At first, he dismissed it and thought that there was something wrong with the way he took stock of his merchandise. But as he began paying more careful attention, he realized that he was missing about a half-dozen eggs each week. He knew that Korolivke had no thieves. The only person who had access to his barn was Wojcik, the peasant who also sold eggs and delivered them to him. During every delivery Shmaysl had been counting them and the numbers were correct. But a day or two later, the number diminished. Shmaysl knew that Wojcik was his competitor, but had no proof that he was responsible for the missing eggs. Knowing that he could not afford to take such losses every week, he went to Rabbi Shimshon for advice:

"Rabbi," Shmaysl said. "I have a problem."

"What's the problem?"

"Someone seems to be stealing eggs from my barn. When I get them delivered, the numbers are correct, and after a couple of days or so, about a half dozen are missing. If this continues, I'll be losing my livelihood. What can I do, Rabbi?"

Rabbi Shimshon was surprised. Stealing in Korolivke? How can that be? Shmaysl assured the rabbi that his story was true. The rabbi thought for a moment:

"I have a solution for you," he said.

"As soon as you get a new delivery, boil a few eggs and put them on top of the egg box which was delivered to you. Whoever comes to steal the eggs must be a dealer because peasants around here have their own chickens that lay eggs. The person who comes to steal them, being in a rush not to be caught, will unknowingly pick up the eggs on top. When those eggs will be sold, the thief will be discovered."

Soon enough, the culprit, his competitor, was caught. The story spread all over Korolivke, and for some reason, Shmaysl received the credit for having solved the problem. Consequently, the shtetl began thinking of him as the wise man of Korolivke.

Shmaysl's Secret

As mentioned, everyone in the shtetl knew Shmaysl. But they only thought they knew him. There were some aspects about his character that he kept to himself; he did not share some dreams with anyone. Shmaysl's small stature and meek appearance belied his inner ambitions. His material needs were secondary to his lifelong dream of reaching higher levels of learning. As a matter of fact, even when he served his customers, he always dressed in a white shirt—a rarity in Korolivke on weekdays—as if he was only temporarily doing his job and would soon leave for a learning session at the synagogue. While he was serving his customers, his eyes looked into the distance as if they were searching for another world. Although he was aware that selling his foods was the only means by which he could earn his livelihood, his desire for learning did not diminish, and his heart longed for the day when he would have enough money to be involved in study.

Perhaps his uncle Zusie from America would someday send him some money so he could realize his dreams. He envisioned himself sitting with the rabbi and other learned men of the shtetl, delving into Talmudic studies and other holy books and uncovering heavenly secrets.

Actually, if not for Shayndl, his wife, he'd have joined long ago the small group of men who met daily before morning prayers to do some learning. But Shayndl was a down-to-earth wife who had no sympathy for her husband's dreams and certainly not the kind of woman to be ignored. She was tiny, edgy and an habitual screamer. She would shout even when she did not know what she was yelling about. She shouted at any opportunity, and seemed to wallow in it. Shayndl was demanding. Her stern voice and the piercing gaze in her eyes when she became angry could make anyone feel that they were about to be attacked by a hungry tigress. It was also Shayndl who had commanded Shmaysl not to even taste a lick of brandy, and Shmaysl knew she was right.

"I had plenty of trouble with you last year with your drinking.," she yelled at him in front of the synagogue on the eve of Purim, and she did it with her index finger pointed so close to his nose that he could smell her cooking. "No more drinking!" she thundered at him with her commanding voice; and she made him swear never to even have a sip of brandy again.

The Liquor Episode

Shmaysl knew that he could not handle alcohol. He also did not forget what had happened to him last Purim. It was a mess.

But this year, at least this year, he was happy. Purim fell on a Sunday. Shmaysl was relaxed after his Sabbath rest the day before. The weather was pleasant and warm. The sky was clear, and the few, tiny white clouds wandered off as if they had decided to leave Korolivke to celebrate Purim under a pure, blue sky.

Shmaysl returned home from the morning service at the synagogue in high spirits. A mild breeze and the pleasant scent from the nearby fields brought a beaming smile to his face. He was in seventh heaven. He had a drink after the morning service and decided that since Purim is only once a year, one must not waste it with material preoccupations. He had momentarily forgotten Shayndl's warning not to ever drink again. Therefore, since Shayndl, may she be blessed, was away handing out Purim presents to friends, he thought he might as well have a drink or two and enjoy a nice Purim nap.

However, as the saying goes: Man plans and God laughs. His plans unexpectedly changed. After a drink or two—actually he could not remember exactly how many—he decided there was nothing that a good nap wouldn't cure. He was about to walk to his bed for a pleasant, comfortable snooze. The problem was that the bed started moving away from him and decided to go into a dance. The room joined in and began whirling around him like a wheel out of control, first slowly, and then faster and faster. He tried with all his strength to stop the room from turning, but to no avail. It is a known fact that after several whiskeys, a person is liable to find out secrets he never knew before. Shmaysl discovered that the room could be just as stubborn as his wife. Not only did the room refuse to stop whirling, it began turning faster as if driven by demons. Shmaysl barely managed to pull himself to open the front door of his house, trying to catch some air, when all hell broke loose.

He could hardly believe his eyes and ears. A gang of imps and ghosts of various sizes, short and long-legged ones, were prancing, jumping, dancing and singing in front of his house. One of them, the tallest, he could swear looked like Ashmedai, the king of demons. He once had a nightmare about him and now he was dancing right in front of him!

"That's all I need now," he said, "no more and no less than the king of the devils!" The thought of it gave him the shivers.

He noticed that human legs were protruding from their weird costumes, but could not be sure, because everything in front of his eyes was turning too fast. Shmaysl did not know what to make of it. "Who ever heard of ghosts prancing around in the middle of the day? And so many of them! Am I just dreaming?" he cried out with alarm. However, everything he saw seemed real. The ghosts pulled Shmaysl into a circle and danced around him, singing:

Shmaysl, Shmaysl
Give us your pickles,
Shmaysl, Shmaysl
Give us your honey.
Shmaysl, Shmaysl
Have no fear.
Give us your goods
And we'll disappear.

"Leave me alone! Leave me alone!" Shmaysl begged the ghosts. "I wanna rest. I'll give you everything I have, but leave me alone!" Shmaysl decided to do everything possible to get rid of them. Suddenly, his uncle Zusye from America came to his mind. May he live a long, healthy life, but when the time will come, he'd surely leave him a nice inheritance, and he, Shmaysl, will, God willing, finally have time to study and no longer have to mess around with sour pickles, horseradish and flies.

He pulled himself together and with great effort made his way to the barrels near the door. It was not an easy task getting to them because the barrels too started dancing as if they suddenly grew feet. He began handing out his delicacies. One ghost with the head of a dog rushed over and had Shmaysl fill up his big pot with sour pickles. Another, a little ox on two feet with three horns, apparently decided not to wait for Shmaysl. He filled himself a huge jar with honey and ran off.

The news that Shmaysl was handing out his goods for free spread like wildfire. It did not take long, and before one could utter the words "may they multiply," that a bunch of housewives descended upon him like a plague of locusts with jars and pots in their hands. To his surprise, the housewives charged at the ghosts who monopolized the barrels. Shmaysl could not understand how the women were not afraid of them. He was always petrified of ghosts and devils. The truth is, he was as scared of these housewives as he was of ghosts. But to have to deal with them and ghosts was more than he could bear! He broke out in a cold sweat and stumbled his way up the ladder to the attic. But the attic too was whirling. The whole world was turning around him with such speed that the floor disappeared from under his feet. He collapsed and fell into a deep sleep.

Sweet Dreams

His sleep was relaxing and sweet. He dreamt that his uncle Zusie from America arrived in town accompanied by the Prince from Lemberg—both riding white horses. His uncle wore a cylinder hat. The village band was playing as they approached his house. Yoine and Fishl showed up in front of his house arguing about the proper procedure for greeting such royal visitors: "I think," said Yoine, "that a prince should be helped down from his carriage. You have to show respect for a prince."

"Nonsense," reacted Fishl with an annoyed grin. "Where is it written that a prince should be helped? He is not sick, is he?"

Shmaysl wasn't happy to see Yoine and Fishl acting out their "weird" arguments but preferred not to get involved with them at such an important moment. The guests dismounted their horses and greeted Shmaysl with royal respect. Shmaysl responded by inviting them to his house. He treated them with Purim delicacies and they praised Shayndl's baking. Shmaysl was pleased and surprised that his uncle called him by his nickname and was informal with him:

"Shmaysl," his uncle said to him, "you can do better than selling sour pickles and horseradish. It's not for you! You are a smart fellow and can do better things." Shmaysl felt wonderful. For the first time someone showed appreciation of him and recognized that he was capable of more than just selling pickles.

"You know, Shmaysl," his uncle continued with a warm tone of voice, "the Prince and I know that you are a very honest fellow, therefore, we would like to offer you a manager's job at our big store in Lemberg."

Shmaysl was in heaven. He felt that he was being offered a chance of a lifetime. Now, he would be making enough money to hire help for his business and put his attention to learning. But to avoid acting undignified, he did not respond to his uncle's spectacular offer with haste and excitement. Instead, he decided to stay calm.

In the meantime, as they were talking, the blue sky turned into a muddy gray, and soon a deluge accompanied by thunder and lightning took place outside. The heavy rain was pouring through the roof into the house and Shmaysl became concerned about his guests.

"Where will I get umbrellas for my distinguished guests," he wondered. "I don't mind getting wet, but how about them? What am I going to do?"

Shmaysl's Awakening

Suddenly, a thunderous sound interrupted his dream. A woman's voice woke him up from his deep sleep. The voice sounded unusually familiar, but he was not awake enough to be able to recognize it immediately. He tried to open his eyes, but they refused to open. Finally, with great difficulty he opened his right eye, and with much effort his left eye followed. He searched for his important guests, but they had disappeared. As he was still lying drenched on the floor he glimpsed at the ceiling and was surprised to see that it was dry. However, when he saw Shayndl standing with a pail over him, he realized where the water came from. He had no idea how long he had been sleeping, but was confident that his wife would, no doubt, with God's help, let him know pretty soon.

"Oy Vey! Look at him stretched out like Prince Pototzki!" Shayndl shouted at him. "May all my enemies have the kind of Purim you gave me!"

"What happened, my wife?" Shmaysl wanted to know, rubbing his half-closed eyes. He began feeling as if someone had been sticking dozens of needles into his head.

"Go down and take a look at your livelihood." Her voice changed momentarily into a devious calm. Shmaysl knew that he was in big trouble, because whenever his wife spoke one sentence with calm, a major storm was brewing in the air.

"What's there to see?" Shmaysl asked.

"Go down, your highness, and you'll find out."

Shmaysl, still half-asleep and soaked, thanks to the pail of water his wife emptied over him, barely managed to make his way down the ladder toward the barrels near the door. When he found them empty, he realized what happened. The ghosts he thought he saw were actually the town's youngsters disguised with masks on their faces in honor of Purim. In spite of his wife's voice getting louder in the background, he was pleased to discover that he was not concerned about the empty barrels. A broad smile lit up his soaked face. He remembered his dream and mumbled to himself:

"A drink is not so bad, and a good dream is better than a sad reality. This was the closest I ever came to becoming a man of learning. Barrels, shmarrels," he chuckled. "Who cares? It was my best Purim ever!"

The Noodnik of Chelm
(A Monologue on Market Street)

Some people call me Leybl the carpenter; others call me Lamed Noodnik. You can call me anything you want; I don't mind. You know what a noodnik is? A noodnik is a bore—a pest. If you think I mind being called noodnik, you are mistaken. I am proud of what I am! If God came down to talk to me, I am sure he would say "Be happy, Leybl, that people call you noodnik. That's what you were born for, my son. Be proud of your title. Some of my best friends are noodniks."

Do you know why I am proud of being a noodnik? Because the world needs people like us. Without us the world would be filled with silent lemishkes.[1]

I see you are twitching your nose and think I am nuts. But just stop and think for a moment. Are you familiar with the Bible? Remember Noah's Ark? If God hadn't wanted to have noodniks in the world, he would not have told Noah to take into his ark "all types." Do you know what He meant by "all types?" He didn't mean only all types of animals. He also meant all types of people, and that includes noodniks too. I may be a carpenter, but I can read between the lines! Carpenters from Chelm are no fools! If God didn't want to have noodniks inside the ark, He would have immersed them in the

1 Milksops—tacit, schlemiels—people who always end up at the wrong end of the stick.

deep waters of the flood without even a "goodbye"—and finished. You would have never heard from them again until the end of time.

So you are smiling, eh?

Just imagine, if the Messiah suddenly came riding on his donkey, looked around and could not find one single noodnik on Earth. Do you know what could, God forbid, happen? I hate to think of it! He would become so shocked, he'd pick himself up and run back to heaven as fast as his feet could carry him. Do you know why? Because the Messiah cannot be without noodniks! He could never live in a world where people don't open their mouths and are afraid to speak up. He needs noodniks—people who are not afraid to talk.

Let me tell you something else. Noodniks speak more truths than most people in this little world of ours. Even a noodnik who is not so wise has a chance to get out some truth... provided, of course, you let him talk long enough. Because once he keeps talking, he'll talk so long until some truth will accidentally come out of his mouth. That's why it is written somewhere that where a noodnik stands, no simple man of flesh and blood can take his place.

Uh... I can see you don't agree. So don't agree! You say it was not written about noodniks? All right... if it isn't written, it should be written! I am sure that when the Messiah will come, noodniks will be the first guests to be invited to the feast of the Leviathan.[2] They will get the most important seats at the table and be served the biggest portions of the fish.

Now, if I ever proved to you that Moses and his brother Aaron belonged to our group and became noodniks by God's command, would you believe me? First, let me tell you... I don't consider myself on the same level with Moses and Aaron. God forbid! I know they were very high-level people, but they still belonged to our brotherhood of noodniks. I can see you asking me where I get such weird ideas. Well, I'll show you. I'll prove to you that what I say is true. They were a part of us and that is a fact!

Remember when God told Moses to go and speak to Pharaoh, and Moses didn't feel like talking? Well, only after God commanded him and Aaron to go and pester Pharaoh again and again to "let my people go," only after they became noodniks—only then—did Moses become the great leader and teacher, and Aaron became a high priest.

---

2 *A sea monster that the righteous will eat at the coming of the Messiah.*

You can be sure: if Moses would not have pestered Pharaoh day after day, we would have never had a chance to even know what matzoh balls are and sit like kings at the Passover Seder. Of course it happened with the help of God. But the point is, God helps people who speak up and are willing to become noodniks.

Now you can see that God has more trust in noodniks than in people who stay silent when they are supposed to talk. He always chose noodniks for His messengers, and He knew what He was doing.

Let me ask you something. Who would have ever known about the prophets if they hadn't pestered the people? They kept talking and talking until someone heard something; and something is better than nothing. Don't you agree? And they still keep on talking to us even after they are gone. Their words sometimes fall on deaf ears, that's true; but they keep on pestering—and that's what makes them noodniks, and that's what makes them special.

You remember how Abraham pestered God and bargained with him to spare Sodom and Gomorrah if He could find 10 righteous people, and God listened to him? Remember? I know you'll ask me: Weren't Sodom and Gomorrah destroyed anyway? Well, I'll answer with another question: Was it Abraham's fault that God couldn't find even 10 decent people there?

My point is, that God listened to Abraham. God lends an ear to people who talk.

Now, please don't misunderstand me! I would never dare to compare myself to our father Abraham, Moses or to the prophets; God forbid! I just want to show you that only talk gets you somewhere. Without talk, one can only get by in the next world but not in this one.

I'll bet you want to know where I got this idea from. What's the matter, you never took a look at the Psalms? Look into the Psalms and you'll see. Here, look! Don't be afraid; it won't bite you! Here! I carry that little Psalm book with me in my pocket all the time, maybe it will bring me luck. It plainly says:

"Neither the dead can praise God, nor the ones who descend in silence," and King David was a pretty smart fellow. To be a king of Jews is not an easy business. They must have driven him crazy with advice, because every Jew, even the poorest, has a wealth of opinions, and they are all perfect.

You know the story of the Jew who came back from a trip to Warsaw full of wonder and told his friends with excitement how many different types of Jews he met; a rightist and a leftist, an Anarchist, a Zionist, an anti-Zionist, an ultra-orthodox and reform Jew, an atheist and an extremely observant conservative Jew.

"Didn't you go on a business trip? How did you find time to meet so many people?" he was asked. "Of course I went shopping to Warsaw," he said. "Then how did you find the time to meet so many people?

"Who said I was talking to many people? You didn't understand me," the man answered restlessly. "I was talking to one Jew!"

So, as I said about David, to be a king of Jews he had to know what he was talking about. If he said that no one prays in the next world, you can believe him!

Now, remember, I have to tell you in all honesty that not every noodnik is a godsend.

Take my competitor, for instance. His name is Mendl the busy mouth. He is a noodnik you wouldn't want to meet. He thinks he's the greatest gift God ever sent down on earth—the greatest genius. He can talk for hours. But the problem is he talks only about one favorite subject—himself. The more he talks, the more he makes a fool of himself. When customers come in to have something fixed, he makes them listen to him until they are ready to faint. And you probably know the saying: Keep your mouth closed and no fly will get in. Mendl does not understand that.

I could tell you stories you won't believe, but I see you are in a rush. Too bad! Remember, nothing good comes from rushing. Don't rush and you'll live longer. As a matter of fact, I know a man who prays very slowly because, he says, the angel of death is not going to get him while he is praying...

So what did I want to tell you? I almost forgot. You know, when you get to my age, the paraphernalia up there in my head begins to behave for some reason in a strange way and gets less and less friendly. Sometimes, one of the instruments up there go on strike; and other times, a few of them decide to go out on strike at the same time as if somebody organized them against me. They act as if I owe them something. You want to know why? Go and ask my limbs why. On second thought, better don't ask them. They won't tell you anyway. Maybe they feel they can do anything they want to an old man. They know I cannot punish them. No respect for older people!

So what did I want to talk to you about? Oh, yes! I remember now. It was about Mendl, my competitor... but you know something? Maybe I shouldn't talk about him the way I do. After all, if God didn't want his type of noodniks around, they wouldn't have been allowed into Noah's ark.

I see you are restless. What's the rush? Everybody I talk to these days is in a big rush. Life is too short!

You are ready to leave? Okay... Okay... I just want you to keep in mind no matter what everyone says, that noodniks are a blessing of God and they are important to the world. But I must be honest with you and warn you: watch out for bad ones! They can bring a man to hell sooner than heaven decides where he should go.

I know it's a sin to talk that way, but God will forgive me. He forgives worse people than me.

I can see, you look like you are standing on needles. Go! Go in peace, I won't stop you. But remember! Nothing good comes from rushing. That's the truth! And remember who told you that! A noodnik told you that! Go in peace with the blessings from the Lamed Noodnik of Chelm.

The Wandering Preacher

Rebbe Zalmen hastened his way to the little prayer house for the Sabbath services. Rushing to perform a mitzvah—a good deed—as one is required, was part of his life's rhythm. He enjoyed coming to Czernowitz; it was his favorite city. Soon, he would be able to share with the worshippers some of his ideas on the Torah readings of the week.

It was a clear, golden summer morning. The trees around the Ring Platz were in full bloom. The rich variety of colors, and the fragrance and beauty of the flowers, overwhelmed his senses. He was not familiar with the names of the various trees and flowers, but had always loved nature and wished it were possible to pray amongst them under the canopy of God's creation. How inspiring that would be! Didn't the holy Baal Shem Tov[1] use special moments for praying in the forest? Our father Isaac prayed in the field. He still remembered the prayer of the Hassidic Master Noson of Breslav:

Master of the Universe, let me seclude myself in prayer... going out in the fields to meditate among the grass and the trees...

---

1 A Jewish mystical rabbi from the 1700s; considered to be the founder of Hasidic Judaism. The term rebbe is used as a title for a Hassidic rabbi. They are interchangeable in this story.

"Of course, buildings are needed as well. But people seem to be inspired more by buildings than by the beauty of nature. Yes, yes... the Holy Temple was a building too. But the Ten Commandments were given on a mountain, not inside a building..."

His thoughts turned to the worshippers in the Little Prayer House, where he was soon going to give his Dvar Torah:[2]

"Some are critical of my thoughts and of my ways of praying," Rebbe Zalmen mused. "Of course, I sometimes get carried away during prayer and become emotional when I don't concentrate enough. At such moments, I am more concerned with the way I relate to God, than with how people see me. People have lost touch with the meaning of prayer. The pious men of old used to prepare themselves for a lengthy period of time before they even began praying in order to direct their hearts toward their Father in Heaven with utmost devotion and concentration. Repeating words mechanically is not praying. Prayer is man's attempt to feel closer to the infinite, and that is a very difficult task for us limited human beings.

"But one must be careful not to challenge people's thinking beyond what they are willing to absorb. It is easier for man to humanize God than to raise himself to higher spiritual levels."

Rebbe Zalmen was in his twenties. He was thin and small-bodied. His beard was black and pointy, and his curious, piercing, lively eyes dominated his face, projecting an energetic and highly spirited person.

He came from a poor family. His father, Zelig, was a tailor in Sadagura, a small town close to Czernowitz. He struggled hard to provide his family with their bare necessities. The rabbi's mother, Riva, was a pious woman. She regretted not having been able to go to school, but promised herself that if she ever had children she would do everything possible to see to it that they became scholars. She made candies and sold them in the local market-place. When Zalmen was born, both father and mother worked for the same purpose: to offer their son a good education. "I want you to be a man of learning," Zelig told his son. So when the boy reached the age of 13, they sent him to the distinguished yeshiva in Lublin. Throughout his years of study, Zalmen would return

---

2 *In this context, remarks pertaining to weekly Torah section.*

home to visit his parents for the holidays. His visits were a time of great joy for them. They were ecstatic when Leib, the local Talmud teacher, told them: "Your son will be a great scholar; you can be very proud of him!"

Zalmen's parents died several months after their son's graduation. Zalmen went through a time of deep sadness but was grateful that his parents lived to see him being ordained and felt that he had accomplished an important part of the commandment Honor Thy Father and Mother. "That is all I waited for," his father had told him before he died. "Now you can go out into the world and teach!" So Zalmen soon began traveling to various towns and villages to preach and thus fulfill his father's dreams.

That is how Rebbe Zalmen became a preacher, albeit without a congregation; a shepherd without a flock—a wandering rabbi. He spoke to young and old from all walks of life, to tailors and teachers, farmers and barbers, to rich and poor. Several times a year he came to give sermons at the Little Prayer House in Czernowitz, but his enthusiasm was always dampened by apprehension whenever he went there. He knew that Czernowitz was quite selective in its choices of preachers and the Little Prayer House was no exception. True, it was only a shtibl, a small-sized prayer room, but its worshippers were a very demanding and critical lot. He felt a negative attitude toward him every time he passed the threshold of the small, narrow door.

He had not preached to its worshippers for some time. But he did remember that after his last sermon several worshippers approached him with questions meant more to challenge him than to look for answers. He was aware that some of the congregants were sympathetic toward him, but still felt uncomfortable with those who were critical of him.

In a way, Rebbe Zalmen could understand them. The late rabbi of the Little Prayer House, who had passed on several years ago, was a holy man and great scholar. His lineage was traceable to the Great Hassidic master, the Rabbi of Rijin. He was a peaceful and wise man. His admirers loved and adored him and could not imagine another rabbi replacing him—not even temporarily. Rebbe

Zalmen's occasional appearances at their prayer house made them uncomfortable, and they considered visits by an "outside" rabbi an imposition into their small circle. They wanted a continuation of their own rabbi's tradition through one of his sons.

At first, they hoped that Rebbe Menahem Ber's oldest son, Nachum, would inherit his father's position, but that was not destined to happen. A year after his father's death, he drowned in the river Prut outside the city.

The next in line, Yaakov, was a talented poet. He had leftist leanings (which later changed as soon as he experienced living under the Soviet regime for one year). He would often be heard arguing that "Religion is not the solution to the problems of humanity." That left Aaron, the youngest son, as next in line to take on the spiritual leadership of the prayer house. The Congregation was elated when Aaron expressed his desire to follow in his father's footsteps. Aaron was a spiritual soul and studious young man, and the worshippers of The Little Prayer House were more than willing to wait for his ordination and assume his father's position, although it would be several years before he could accept this position.

Rebbe Zalmen found out about Rabbi Ber's passing and the congregants' decision to wait several years for the youngest son to inherit his father's position. He felt that a house of prayer must not be left for a long period of time without spiritual guidance, and that it was his responsibility to make occasional visits to the Little Prayer House. He did not care about remuneration. He knew the little synagogue could not pay him for his visits. The little income they received from contributions went toward replacing the old, torn prayer books and installing a new security door. Times were changing and a synagogue needed security.

•   •   •   •

Czernowitz was considered a modern city in the surrounding areas. Even architecturally it boasted a degree of sophistication. It was often referred to as Little Vienna. It was a city of diverse cultures, and so was its Jewish cultural life. Great Hassidic rabbis and their followers established their residences there. It produced writers and musicians, atheists and freethinkers, communists and socialists, anarchists, Yiddishists, Zionists and anti-Zionists. It combined the simplicity of old Eastern Europe with the more modern living style of the West and became a prominent Jewish cultural center. The first World Yiddish Congress took place there. Great artists like Musician George Enescu would come to give performances at the philharmonic building. The city produced the Jewish poet Paul Celan, the writer Josef Burg, the poets Eliezer Steinberg, Itzik Manger, Yaakov Friedman and others. They lived and wrote in this city. Joseph Schmidt, one of the greatest tenors of his time, also came from the area. In short, it was a city, Rebbe Zalmen felt, ideally suited for his visits. "Culture will not save the world," he said with frustration in his voice. "The world needs God to save man from man."

Rebbe Zalmen looked at his watch. It was ten minutes to nine. Two more streets and he will be at the Little Prayer House in time for the beginning of the services. He did not wish to arrive too early because one is not supposed to engage in idle talk before prayers. "Why don't they like my ideas," he wondered. "They may not be used to my ways of thinking but I always put at the center of my talks Halachic[3] principles and approach everyone with Derech Eretz.[4] True, I sometimes bring up thoughts they might not like. But at least they deserve being listened to."

He felt, for instance, that prayers requiring worshippers to stand should not be protracted by cantors or others who lead prayers. "At such times they have a captive audience," he complained. "Don't they realize that some people find it difficult to stand for a prolonged period of time? 'Tircha D'tzibura'[5]...remember? One must not cause undue hardships to the public!"

He approached Cantor Raphael and suggested to him that it would be helpful not to prolong their singing at such prayers like Kedusha.[6] Raphael had a fine and powerful baritone, and his ego was not inferior to his voice. He expressed his annoyance with the Rabbi's idea:

3 Legal matters.
4 Consideration of others.
5 Aramaic expression meaning discomfort to the public.
6 A prayer requiring one to stand up while reciting it.

"For hundreds of years cantors have been saving their voices for those special prayers and you want us to ignore our favorite liturgical melodies?" he asked Rebbe Zalmen.

Rebbe Zalmen's Manner of Praying

Rebbe Zalmen had a unique way of praying which some congregants found strange and undignified. He knew that his emotional and even restless way of praying was not liked by some people. "Why should it matter to them if I raise my arms to God?" he wondered. True, he sometimes banged his fist impatiently against his prayer book stand, or walked restlessly back and forth during prayers. "Does praying with emotion make me a bad rabbi?"

However, some people were not used to his mannerisms.

"Whoever heard of a rabbi clenching his fist and banging it on the table ... and to make it worse, during prayer?"

In addition, they were also annoyed when they saw him playfully making funny faces at the children after prayers, encouraging them to do the same.

"...And how do you like his fooling around with children? He acts like he is one of them. That's terrible!" people grumbled.

The rabbi's appearance seemed to also be an issue for them.

"How do you like the way he dresses? It is not becoming for a rabbi."

His caftan was at times unevenly buttoned so that one side came out longer than the other. But that did not bother Rebbe Zalmen.

"It's true that I am sometimes forgetful and careless with the way I dress. But when I see the misery in God's world, I am very upset and buttons are the last thing on my mind."

To those who liked him, his dress could not distract them from his large, round, intense black eyes, which focused with discerning awareness and razor-sharp precision on his listeners. They liked his sermons on Musar[7] and Halacha.[8] "What more important subjects can there be to talk to people about than ethical living, matters of the soul and law," they reasoned.

It is said, perhaps with some measure of exaggeration, that in any given synagogue, opinions exceed the number of worshippers. For

7 *Teaching of ethics.*
8 *Matters of law.*

those sharing this view, the Little Prayer House fitted that description. Both sides—the pros and cons—were equally convinced of their respective positions. A considerable part of the congregation, however, had no sympathetic feelings towards the rebbe. They felt that a rebbe is supposed to carry himself with dignity, and that Rebbe Zalmen acted in an "undignified manner."

"Never mind what he thinks or says. First he must act like a rebbe."

"And how do you think a rebbe should act? Do you have a prescription for rabbinical behavior?"

"Never mind your joking!" was the answer.

Some simply refused to open themselves up to the rebbe's sermons and continued to react against his "strange behavior" with groans of dissatisfaction and caustic remarks while calling him by an unusual nickname: The Wild One—a most unheard-of epithet to be thrown at a man of God.

The youngsters' opinion about the Rebbe was quite different. The same characteristics that bothered the adults gave the children pleasure. They liked him. No matter how outlandish he appeared to his critics, the children were the rebbe's most beloved admirers. In their eyes, he was their hero. He was on their side. Like them, he was spontaneous, nimble-bodied and high-spirited. They saw the frowns on the faces of some of the adult worshippers as they glared with mocking smiles at the rebbe's "wild behavior" and occasional fist-banging on his lectern during prayer, but that did not matter to the children. They knew that the rebbe did not bang his fist out of anger. All the discourteous looks and disparaging comments directed against him could not prevent the children from liking him. They were attracted to his personality and liveliness and knew that he liked them. His vitality and animated style of praying proved to them that even a rebbe could be like them, and that there is no need to fear being lively in a house of prayer. They didn't like being reprimanded by their parents for "running around like street boys." Why, they wondered, should they have to sit pasted to their benches when the rebbe doesn't consider it a sin to be lively? But the parents chided their children. "A synagogue should not be a place for wild behavior; not for children and not for a rebbe."

For some reason, the children referred to Rebbe Zalmen as The Tall One. One might wonder why children would think of someone as "tall" when he actually was considerably small in stature? Well, children have their own standards by which they measure grown-ups. Perhaps his oversized black caftan and huge round black hat may have had something to do with it. Or, perhaps, it might have been his disproportionately long arms, which he stretched out towards heaven during his prayers. (In that Little Prayer House, his heaven-bound gestures amounted to touching the ceiling.)

It stands to reason that whenever Rebbe Zalmen visited the synagogue, the tempo of the children's prayers underwent a considerable acceleration process. They tried to conclude each prayer ahead of everyone else, so as to give their prying eyes more time to watch the rebbe. And watch him they did with owlish eyes, filled with childish curiosity and delight.

"Look at the rebbe," they whispered into each other's ears with joyful excitement whenever Rebbe Zalmen would pace around or make one of his restless motions. It was lots of fun watching him. Even the older boys, who did not want to be associated with the younger ones because of their age difference, were not embarrassed to show their pleasure as they watched him with fascination. They joined in the fun, returning the funny faces the rebbe playfully made at them.

Both the big folk—their negative views of the rebbe notwithstanding—and the little folk did share one thing in common, albeit for different reasons: Both sides found themselves more absorbed by Rebbe Zalmen's spontaneous personality and appearance than with the content of his sermons.

Menashe, the Critic

The most outspoken critic of Rebbe Zalmen was the shoemaker in the synagogue, Menashe. Menashe was a small-sized man in his forties with eagle-like eyes, for whom anger was as normal as breathing. Although he wore special shoes with raised heels, he found it necessary to stand on his toes when he was angry, and that was most of the time. It must have made him feel more important, or taller, or both. The more anger he expressed, the more honest he felt. Talking to Menashe peacefully and quietly was a thankless task. He respected volume, and reason was a quality of which he was the sole owner. Menashe considered anyone with a kind disposition and smile on their face a hypocrite.

"Look at that smile," he fumed while his voice was quivering with rage, "What is he so happy about, that stupid good-for-nothing?"

Actually, if Menashe had had his way naming everyone in town, his substitute for everyone's family name would have been "stupid." And it should not come as a surprise. He had a little extra anger stashed away in his heart for everybody and was very even-handed about it. There was not one group of "stupid people" or "hypocrites"; everyone belonged to the same class and was treated equally.

Menashe's philosophy of life was based on his experience with shoes. "People are like hard shoes," he would growl. "They only understand something if you nail it into their heads."

Once, someone approached Menashe and asked him: "Menashe, if you are so unhappy with the Rebbe's sermons and his praying, why don't you talk to him about it?"

At this question, Menashe became indignant and burst out with anger: "You are asking me why I don't walk over and talk to Rebbe Zalmen; is that what you are asking me?" Increasing his anger another few degrees, he repeated the question again: "You really want to know why I don't talk to Rebbe Zalmen? Well, I'll tell you why, you brainless creature! Do you think he would understand me? I'll bet you never thought of that, did you? I said it before and I'll say it again: He shouldn't be a rebbe. He doesn't act like a rebbe and he doesn't talk like a rebbe! That's all!" And as if to add more importance to his statement, he walked off boiling with anger.

But two small groups, sympathetic to Rebbe Zalmen, defended him—each for their own reasons: One group would have taken any stand just to be refuting Menashe; the other really liked Rebbe Zalmen.

"Why do you pay attention to his mannerisms and not to his talks?" they complained to the rabbi's critics. "He has many good things to say. Did you forget that the *Wisdom of the Fathers* teaches not to judge a jug by its appearance but by its contents?"

Unfortunately, the rebbe's sympathizers were too small in number to effect a change in attitude among his critics.

Although he was quite aware of the worshippers' sentiments toward him, Rebbe Zalmen did not wish to reproach them for their behavior toward him. It was not proper, he felt, to use his sermons as a personal appeal on his own behalf.

"The problem is that they don't know me," he said with sadness. "If they bothered to get to know me, they would better understand my preoccupation with more important things than buttons or my way of praying. If they had only been willing to remember their own rebbe's talks, they would behave differently."

Rebbe Zalmen remembered hearing one of the late Menahem's sermons, during which he spoke on a quotation from the Talmud regarding not judging a person until or unless one finds himself in the same situation. He remembered the rabbi talking about spiritual numbness and lack of compassion. "People's emotions are often easier stirred by some superficial matter than by a human being's pain." One would think that because of the high regard they had for their spiritual leader, they would remember his messages and take them to heart. "But then, why should I single out these people," he thought. "All over the world, superficiality fills the vacuum that emanates from inner emptiness."

Rebbe Zalmen knew, of course, of Menashe's negative feelings towards him and felt sad that he could not find a way to communicate with him. "The poor man does not look beyond his shoes," he thought. Rebbe Zalmen was aware that his sermons didn't reach everyone and that many people were not receptive to his ideas. There were times when he was filled with doubts about the effectiveness of his mission. Perhaps, he thought, his sermons were too complex and lack clarity. After all, the Torah had been written in simple language—in the tongue of man. "Perhaps," he thought, "there is a lesson for me to be learned here."

At times he would even question his readiness to preach:

"Who are you, Rebbe Zalmen, to preach to others when you have so much to learn yourself?" he reproached himself. "But someone has to do this work. I must not allow myself to be disillusioned. Even Moses, the great teacher, had his troubles. Did he give up when he came down the mountain with the tablets and found the multitude worshipping a golden calf? If Moses had to put up with problems, who am I to complain?"

"No, no," the rebbe mused. "I must not be impatient. Because of my impatience I cannot find peace—not even during my prayers..."

Rebbe Zalmen's eyes caught a group of children who had just run into the prayer house. "Children, ah ... children, they are marvelous! They are closer to God than any of us adults; and it's no wonder. They have spent less time on earth." He could still remember the time when he was a yeshiva boy and would earn a little pocket money tutoring children. What a joy it was to hear their questions, their pure unadulterated approach to everything around them! Yes, he loves children and he knows they feel it, especially when he winks at them during their boisterous moments.

That love affair was a mutual one, and it made the children feel good to be accepted and liked by this learned man. Yet, in spite of the way the children felt about him, none of them ever dared approaching the rebbe to satisfy their curiosity about his unusual way of praying. They were hoping for an opportune moment that would, eventually, provide them with an answer. A year later, and after much grumbling from the adults, that moment finally arrived.

One Saturday morning, on his next visit to the Little Prayer House, the children overheard that Rebbe Zalmen was in the city and would be visiting the synagogue. They were eager to meet him before he entered the synagogue. Stefanie Gasse—the street where the Little Synagogue stood—was narrow, paved with cobblestones and had little traffic, so the congregants felt comfortable letting their children play outside. That gave the children a chance to meet Rebbe Zalmen before he would enter the synagogue. Adjoining the Stefanie Gasse (street) was a plaza. Knowing that Rebbe Zalmen would arrive from that direction, they hurried out to the end of the block, waiting for him. It could not be too long before he would arrive, because the prayers begin at nine o'clock and it was already five minutes before. Anyway, it didn't matter how long they would have to wait. They looked forward to greeting him. Besides, he often had candies for them. It didn't take long. His figure appeared in the distance and they ran towards him with a kind of happiness only children know.

Mendl, The Noodle, being one of the older Heder[9] boys, decided to be the one daring to see the rebbe after the prayers and question him about his way of praying. Mendl's nickname had its reason. He was rather small for his nine years and his physical presence gave one more the impression of a stick than a child's body; so much so, that it was quite easy to think of him as a shrunken noodle. His face had an asymmetry communicating that God's generosity does not necessarily always come accompanied with blessings. Or, to put it differently, God's bounty may sometimes be too generous for the human eye to appreciate. His large-rimmed eyeglasses covered a large part of his elongated, pale face and hung awkwardly over his thinly shaped nose, constantly threatening to desert it, winding up invariably on its tip. It was an unending battle in which the glasses always lost. His walk was studied and carefully planned. He always paced his steps in a slow, stately fashion while stiffening his thin body. This he apparently did out of respect for the much revered biblical scholar and his idol, Mr. Efros, who lived across the street from Mendl's home, and a man whom Mendl was intensely anxious to emulate. Mr. Efros had been plagued by severe arthritis and had been walking sluggishly for several years. Replicating Mr. Efros' walk made Mendl feel close to, if not in, the scholar's league. It must not be left out here that Mendl the Noodle was not an average student. He was considered the scholar of the Heder because of his encyclopedic knowledge of the Pentateuch. Perhaps it might be more correct to say that he was more of a visiting scholar, due to his frequent bouts of illnesses that kept him from attending Heder regularly.

Actually, Mendl was not always called by his nickname. True, when it came to games, he was referred to as Noodle:

"Hey Noodle, how do you expect to run with us? You'll collapse." Or, "Face it, Noodle; you can't throw darts. Better go home and read books!"

But when it came to problems requiring his encyclopedic brain, their attitudes toward him changed. In times of need he was addressed as Mendl, and his information was much cherished. Whenever a fellow classmate needed answers to questions like "Who was Hanoch?" or "What was Rashi's[10] comment on the Red Heifer?"

9 *Elementary school for religious studies.*
10 *Medieval commentator.*

Mendl had the answer ready, as if pulled out from a special file. And on Fridays, when the class was tested with tricky questions on the reading of the week, a little note from Mendl with the answer slipped under the table to the nervous, queried and perspiring classmate was a much welcomed relief.

Mendl was no fool. He was aware that favors can be easily forgotten. He also understood that his colleagues needed him for the answers just as much as he needed them for his playmates. So he decided to resort to the power of bargaining in order to get to play in their games. Friday was the best day for that. When the boys gathered outside the Heder with nervous anticipation before their weekly test, Mendl felt on top of the world. He knew that in moments like these he had the upper hand. "If you want me to help you with the answers, you better let me play in the games; otherwise, forget it!" His classmates had to agree.

Mendl Confronts the Rebbe

On that Sabbath, when Mendl the Noodle decided to gather his courage and question Rebbe Zalmen about his unusual way of praying, Menashe the Shoemaker found out about it and became furious.

"Can you imagine the hutzpah[11] of that shrunken good-for-nothing, trying to talk to the rebbe? Who does he think he is? That's the job of an older person, not that little shrunken snail."

But another side of him felt quite relieved. Menashe was not the sort of fellow who tolerated dialogues. He knew that he wouldn't feel comfortable entering into a discussion with Rebbe Zalmen. Now no one would bother asking him why he, himself, didn't confront the rebbe with his complaints. "Let the Noodle do it," he told himself with a sense of relief.

However, not to allow his anger to dissipate completely, he kept repeating: "What hutzpah! That shrunken good-for-nothing... Can you imagine?"

After the services had ended, Mendl showed signs of approaching the rebbe. Menashe immediately trotted after the boy. Quickly a group of curious worshippers could be seen trailing along behind them. Mendl stood at a short distance away from Rebbe Zalmen,

11 Nerve.

waiting for the right moment to approach him. Watching the rebbe with nervous anticipation as he was about to cross the threshold and exit the prayer house, Mendl decided that there was no time to lose. He darted towards Rebbe Zalmen with the eagerness of a squirrel running toward a nut... but not without some anxiousness. However, as nervous as he was, he also felt quite pleased with himself for having summoned the courage to speak to the rebbe. He tried to tighten his tie, wipe his nose and clear his throat—none with much success. While mumbling a greeting, Mendl came straight to the point and spilled out his well-prepared question to the rebbe with nervous speed and in a staccato manner sprinkled with a mild, goat-like stutter:

"Re-e-e-be," he said in a half-choked voice that seemed to have propelled itself involuntarily out of his throat with a high-pitched voice he himself could not recognize. "Uh... Rebbe, we-e-e saw you bang your fist during prayers. We are...uh...a-a-all very uh...curious t- t- t- to know w---hy you do that... Uh... we learned uh... that God knows what we th-th--ink. So why, uh...then do you p-p-pray as if God has tr-rr-ouble hearing?"

A lighthearted smile appeared on the rabbi's face. He was glad to have been given an opportunity to explain his feelings, and especially happy that it was a child who approached him with that question. Although he didn't seem surprised by the question, it did nevertheless take him a moment to gather his thoughts.

Having observed Menashe standing in the circle of people who followed Mendl, Rebbe Zalmen decided to say a few words directed indirectly at Menashe too. The rebbe straightened out his restless body as if preparing for a task, and in his customary, lively manner addressed the boy:

"My dear young fellow, the fists have no part in my praying. I use them in frustration when my mind cannot stay silent and wanders off into the darkness of empty and meaningless thought. Perhaps, when Reb Menashe compares a human being to a hard shoe, he may have something there. We human beings are somewhat like hard shoes when it comes to opening ourselves up to the world of the spirit. The comparison, however, is not complete. A hard shoe can be handled with an appropriate nail. Another good thing about a shoe is that if it is hard, it will not try to convince you that it is soft. Unfortunately, there is no equivalent for nails when it comes to the human brain and heart. A human being is more complex than that. We were given the ability to think—a blessing we don't frequently make use of."

"What we need to arrive at," he continued with a meditative look in his eyes gazing somewhere into the far distance, "is a state in which the *Ani*, the I, transcends into *Ain*—a state of nothingness. It is only through such a state that we can enter the realm of the spirit through which the Eternal speaks to us. When the I assumes importance, our receptivity becomes feeble. To become receptive to matters of the spirit, a first requirement is inner stillness without the I in the way."

Rebbe Zalmen noticed Menashe moving restlessly and making grimaces.

"Silence," he said, "preceded the word in the process of creation. Silence is God's first-born, so to speak, and takes precedence over language. Language is limited but peaceful silence seems to be the secret passageway to man's soul. The prophet Elijah once said: God is not in the whirlwind or in the earthquake or in the fire but in the still, small voice that speaks within the human soul. I am searching for that still voice. When I feel that my mind is not quiet and chatters away without stop, I get very impatient with myself. We are taught to seek peace and pursue it. It is in there, in the silence of our inner chamber, where the true eternal spirit dwells and where one can find peace and a closer relationship with the Divine. I believe that God is receptive to all. When I will achieve a greater receptivity to Him, you will surely see me pray with more calm and peace. My apologies to you, young fellow, for having created the wrong impression. If anyone has trouble hearing, it is not God but I. A good and peaceful Sabbath to you, my son."

With his usual, bouncy step he took off and faded gradually into the distance. The boys crowded around Mendl, wanting to know what the Rebbe said.

"Hey, Mendl, what did Rebbe Zalmen mean?"

"There's no point telling you, 'cause you wouldn't understand anyway."

Mendl was quite pleased seeing that the boys once again came to him for help. It made him feel needed. Actually, he had some trouble himself understanding the rebbe... all that stuff about silence of the inner chamber...what did he mean by that? But, of course, he would not tell the boys that he too had trouble with the rebbe's explanation. "Let them continue to depend on me," he mumbled to himself with great satisfaction.

As far as the worshippers were concerned, they—at least most of them—began having second thoughts about Rebbe Zalmen and feel that there may be more to him than his mannerisms.

"What did Rebbe Zalmen mean by his talk," one worshipper asked.

"Could be he means," tried to guess another, "that we were unjustly nasty towards him."

"Maybe he is a Lamed-Vovnik[12]" came a shaken voice from the crowd with awe.

"Never mind Lamed-Vovniks," interjected his neighbor impatiently, "maybe what it amounts to is that we better take a mirror and look in front of our own noses so we can better see ourselves first, before we criticize a man like Rebbe Zalmen."

"It looks like we were wrong about him," confessed another apologetically. "One must not judge a jug by its appearance but by its contents," added another, repeating mechanically what the rebbe's sympathizers had been saying all along.

"Maybe we should be more critical about our own praying rather than be busy with how Rebbe Zalmen prays," muttered quietly another.

... And Menashe? Menashe, of course, he was boiling with anger. He directed his fury at Rebbe Zalmen:

"Did you ever hear a thing like that, did you? Did you hear him talk about shoes?" he asked the crowd angrily. "What business does he have to talk about shoes? What does he know about shoes?" The people around him smiled. He looked like he was angry at himself.

An interesting change, however, took place but went unnoticed. When Rebbe Zalmen left, his walk had the usual lively bounce, but for some reason it was more peaceful.

---

12 According to tradition, there are at least 36 holy people through whose goodness the world is sustained.

Judgment Day

Dreams can carry us to realms beyond our physical reach.

In this dream, it was the end of Yom Kippur,[1] during the closing prayer of Neila[2]—when, according to tradition, the gates of Heaven are closing and the sentences for every human being's fate are being sealed. I was standing before the awesomely feared Heavenly Court. Time seemed of no consequence. There was only an awareness that I had reached the moment at which every human being eventually arrives.

Floating in the background of the enormous throne in the Court of Judgment on High, were the gigantic tablets of the Ten Commandments. The writing on the tablets was intermingled with tens, perhaps hundreds of thousands, of small letters surrounding them in a seemingly perpetual flutter.

"Can you read these small letters?" A stern voice was directed at me from the judgment chair. Eagerly, and with some degree of confidence, I began reading, but soon discovered that neither my perception nor my vision were as clear as I thought they were on Earth.

1 Day of Atonement.
2 Final service of Yom Kippur
(The Closing of the Gates).

"I am trying to make them out, but my vision is blurred," I said with considerable hesitation.

"We have heard that before," said the voice. "Now, who are you and what is your name?" The voice became sterner.

"I am sure, Your Eternal Highness, you have more information about me than I could ever provide." I said in a fearful tone of voice.

"Here, we don't ask questions out of ignorance. Memory is infinite and absolute. We know who you are. You are being tested to see whether *you* know who *you* are!"

I gave them my name and my profession.

"Are you aware that what you do has nothing to do with who you are? You are now in the world of truth! People are not judged here by the status they have or have not achieved in their lives but by what they have accomplished in good deeds. You had better understand that!"

"I understand, Your Honorable Highness."

"Now, let's get on with your actual deeds. What did you accomplish in your lifetime?"

"Well, I worked hard, although I must admit to some degree of laziness..." I added, with some inflection of guilt.

"You mean, you squandered the faculties given to you," the voice chided me. I was attempting to make a case in my defense, so I continued:

"I studied to improve at my profession hoping to be of use to society, trying to be a better person, and..."

I was interrupted. "Everyone is hoping and trying to become better instead of being better. People don't seem to realize that hoping and trying are prevarications. What is there to try? When you wanted food, you did not try to eat? As long as you had food available, you ate, didn't you? Choice is not a matter of time, of trying and hoping, but of will and action."

There was an uncomfortable pause.

"I guess you are right," I said sheepishly, cringing from embarrassment. Hoping to somewhat improve the critical atmosphere, I added something I thought would turn in my favor:

"To make up for time lost during the war years, I tried to study a tiny portion of your holy writings. Unfortunately, I could not spend as much time as I would have wanted to. I had to plan and prepare myself for a self-supporting life. After all, isn't it said that the ideal life is 'Torah V'avoda'—learning and work?"

"Well, look at that, we have a regular lawyer here! And for what purpose did you study the holy writings?"

I was completely baffled and at a loss for words. "Isn't it considered a mitzvah[3] to study Torah for its own sake?" I said, with a tentative mumble.

The voice came thundering at me. "'For its own sake does not mean studying without a purpose. The holy writings were not given to man to be studied for the sake of mental exercise and entertainment. Its application to life is its purpose. The meaning of the Bible becomes alive only through its practice. It is a Torat Chaim.[4] Tell us how you applied the little you learned?"

"As best as I could."

The voice continued its stern tone. "That is not a good enough answer! People are very selective in how they apply the holy writings. They go through the motions of following them, and when it comes to inner change, they prefer to resort to prayer, asking the Eternal One to do their work for them. Instead of following the commandments, they get more stuck on symbols, which seem to be getting greater attention than their intrinsic value. If you point a finger toward a certain direction, they concentrate on the finger rather than on the direction. And when they study the holy writings, they often take pride in quoting them but not as often do they really live by the principles they represent."

I had no answer. It sounded true; I decided that I better stay silent.

"Well... what do you have to say for yourself? You know what we mean. Don't act dumb! This is not the earthly circus with people playing their silly games of trying to fit God into their small-size brains through exercises in intellectual acrobatics. You must realize that this is no place for pretense. Remember, you are in the World of Truth now!"

Again, there was a pause. I decided that silence is more than golden at this point.

"I see you made your living in music."

"Yes, Your Highness," I said, not without pride.

3 A good deed.
4 A Torah relevant to life.

"Were you comfortable to fiddle and make music while the world was—and still is—burning?"

"Your Highness! With all due respect and all modesty, I must say something that has been bothering me for a long time. It is about the angels. Am I wrong in assuming that angels sing in the heavens while tragedies are happening on earth, and while there is so much pain, hunger, suffering and misery?   Isn't there a commentary that while the Egyptians were drowning in the sea as they were pursuing the Israelites, the angels were about to be jubilant and sing, and the Eternal One admonished them saying: 'My creatures are drowning in the sea and you want to sing'?

"I had experienced more than my share of pain on earth and simply missed death because the murderers didn't have enough time to get to me. My father and so many in the pious, beautiful world I grew up in did not survive. I was a child at that time and had lost the desire to live after losing Father. But, somehow, after some time—although time did not heal my pain—I felt that I had to go on.

"No! I don't feel guilty for having occupied my life searching for music. After much pain and crying, I decided to look for the positive rather than concentrating on my sorrows. I did it through music— a field in which I was granted some measure of ability. In all modesty, Your Eternal Highness, perhaps you would kindly grant me the wisdom to understand why your messengers were allowed to sing praises in Heaven, and I, a helpless child at the time who tried with all my strength to overcome my pain and forget my injuries and all the injustices I experienced, should have shied away from beauty? It seems to me that there is greater sadness on Earth than in heaven. Heaven, we are told, has no illnesses, no suffering and no murder. It seems to me that there is much greater need for music on Earth than in heaven. Please tell me if I am wrong," I continued in a pleading voice. "I am sure I made many mistakes on Earth, but occupying my life with music was not one of them."

I felt a deadly silence and hoped that what I said might, perhaps, have touched an agreeable chord with the Court of Heavenly Justice. But I could not tell for certain. There were other arrivals who were going through the same questioning and seemed to fare worse than I did. Thousands upon thousands of newly arriving souls were thoroughly and intensely questioned. There we all stood waiting together, sinner and saint in the celestial corridors, somewhere between the awesome gates of heaven and hell in complete ignorance of our future fate. No soul ever doubted that a final verdict based on perfect heavenly justice would be accompanying each and everyone into eternity and be meted out in a clear, resounding, powerful manner.

Instead, an eerie silence enveloped us. It seemed to last forever. Perhaps that silence had its own voice and language, but its meaning was incomprehensible.

I stood in bewilderment wondering why no perceptible answer came from the Throne of Heavenly Justice, whose questioning had been so demanding and strict with me and the other arriving souls. With eagerness, anxious anticipation and some trepidation, I awaited to finally experience Eternal Truth in its entire majestic splendor. I was ready to accept my retribution whatever that might be, as long as others and those who created misery on Earth also received theirs. But the only response was that of an incomprehensible, mysterious silence.

There was nothing for me left to do but wait for an intelligible answer. I could wait; I had all the time. After all, I was in a World of Timelessness.

The Professor and the Tailor
(A Dialogue)

Characters: Dr. Bailey, Mr. Green, Mrs. Green.

The setting is a park in the Bronx, on a clear, summer Sunday morning. Dr. Bailey, a retired professor of philosophy, is sitting on a bench engrossed in a book. He is interrupted by an unexpected greeting from his neighbor, Mr. Green, a tailor.

Mr. Green walks over to Dr. Bailey's bench with careful steps, trying not to disturb him, and greets the professor.

MR. GREEN: A good morning to you, professor.

DR. BAILEY: Good morning, Mr. Green.

MR. GREEN, hesitantly: Am I interrupting you? I see you are in the midst of reading. What is it you are reading? I'll bet, another book on philosophy or psychology, maybe religion? Am I right?

DR. BAILEY: You are right, my friend. Step into my office. Would you like to sit down?

MR. GREEN: Thanks, professor. Don't mind if I do.

He sits down, makes himself comfortable on the bench and addresses the professor:

MR. GREEN: It's nice to have a good education and be able to read high-caliber books, be knowledgeable in philosophy and psychology. I would give away an arm for the chance to have had a better education, but, unfortunately, I had to grow up without much schooling. The little I learned dates back to my very early childhood, you know. But that does not stop me from thinking; no, sir! In my rare quiet moments, I manage to throw away my worries and indulge in a little pondering about the world, politics, and even God.

DR. BAILEY: That is quite commendable. I hope you make some interesting discoveries. (*Laughingly*) So far, I haven't achieved much success in these areas.

MR. GREEN: Perhaps you might wonder why a simple tailor like me occupies his mind with things other than my trade. Well, some people feel that their trade is the most important thing in their lives, and I can understand that. After all, a person has to eat. But I don't think that's enough. I feel that if people don't care about what's going on around them, they won't need their profession, because there won't be a world. And as far as God is concerned, well, God has been on my mind since I can remember, and it fascinates me to see how He runs the world. I hope He has some good plans for it before we humans mess it up so badly that the curses in the Bible will look mild in comparison with the horrors we will cause each other. It could become so bad that God himself wouldn't recognize the world He created...

Pauses for a second or two.

I'm just kidding, of course. I know, I am talking about God as if He would be a family member of mine. I hope He will forgive me. Where I come from, God is almost like family. Every move we make is related to God's dos and don'ts, so we get to think of Him as sort of a close relative.

DR. BAILEY (*Thoughtfully*): That's all right. Millions of people adopted a more or less similar concept of God! It certainly is one way of trying to deal with the unknown. We poor humans don't have much more available to us but the narrow tunnels of our limited vision. Through these scanty passageways we manage to carve out an individualized concept of God that matches only our woeful limitations of understanding the universe.

MR. GREEN (*Meditatively*): I could not think of God being too far away when I need help. For me, He must be personal and nearby; otherwise, who am I going to turn to when I am in trouble? Besides, if flowers are blooming and people are born, God must be here— right here—as we talk. How can people live happily in a state of isolation, without feeling that God is all around us? Maybe the reason some poor lost souls in those cults who committed group suicide chose to die together was because they did not feel that God is everywhere, near them, around them. It must be a very lonely feeling not to feel that God and life go together.

DR. BAILEY: During my lifetime, I have come to realize that the concept of being isolated from a God, who is somewhere in Heaven, is an invention of the human mind. You cannot feel isolated when you feel at one with all of creation. If you believe that God is everywhere, it is not a question of how close God is to you, but how close you are to God's creation?

Mrs. Green passes by with two shopping bags in her hands.

MR. GREEN (*Looks up and sees his wife approaching*): Here comes my wife. She is a good wife and has a good nature. She takes good care of our children. But when she hears me philosophizing or talking about books, she gets irritated.

I guess she feels I should concentrate more on making a better living. I can't blame her for that. But is it my fault that I am not good in business? I cannot explain that to her.

MRS. GREEN (*Approaches them and waits until her husband finishes talking*): Good morning, professor. Is my husband bothering you again? I heard what he said to you. I keep telling my husband that if a person puts his mind to something and keeps at it, he can be successful, and we really need to increase our income. It won't come from his reading books. You know, since he has been paying attention to books he is not himself anymore. He started sounding like a lawyer, or a philosopher—those people that make a living using funny words and accomplish nothin'.

DR. BAILEY (*Amused, answers good-naturedly*): I am one of those guilty ones.

MRS. GREEN (*Somewhat embarrassed*): But you make a living from it!

(*She turns to Mr. Green, pointing an accusatory finger at him*): Don't bother the professor and don't be late for lunch.

(*She walks away awkwardly*)

MR. GREEN: I don't know what's wrong with being educated. I hope someday I will be able to read the books you read. My wife says that she married me when I talked like a schlemiel and she doesn't mind if I stay that way. She isn't interested, she says, in my philosophizing or in my grammar. She is only interested in one thing, she says: I should make a living. Isn't it written somewhere that "Man does not live by bread alone"? But how can you explain that to my wife? If there are some people I can't understand, my wife is certainly one of them.

He stops for a moment, makes sure he has the professor's attention, and continues:

I know you might ask why I didn't study more in my youth if I like education so much. Well, life hasn't been easy. You see, since I was 14 years old, I had to be the breadwinner in my family, and now that I am getting older, nothing has changed except my age. I am still struggling to make a living, and I guess until the last day of my life I'll continue my battle to provide for my family's needs.

Not that I am complaining, you understand. God forbid! I am counting my blessings. My family is in good health. True, my older daughter just went through a bad skin rash (and an expensive one too), and my youngest had the measles this year. But I know that such things are part of life and it would be silly of me to complain. We must be reasonable. Everyone must get their share of troubles, so why should my family be different? We cannot ask God to be unfair and assign someone else the troubles he assigned for us. Right?

DR. BAILEY (*With a mischievous smile*): I am discovering a sense of humor in you.

MR. GREEN: Outside my troubles, I also have problems with my oldest daughter.
(He stops for a moment and continues):
It looks to me like nowadays a parent must have more knowledge of the world to be able to handle his children. Take for instance my older daughter. She says we are old-fashioned and don't adjust to modern life. She sees movies my wife and I would be ashamed to see. I am not saying she is a bad girl, but in my time and where I come from, a girl who dressed the way she dresses and goes to the places she goes would have been considered an outcast. She pays a little more money just so her jeans would have holes in them. What a generation! I can't understand that!

DR. BAILEY: Have you ever heard of Khalil Gibran?

MR. GREEN: No, I never did.

DR. BAILEY: He said something I consider interesting, although you might not agree with him. He said, and I will try to quote for you from memory:

"Your children are not your children.
They are sons and daughters of Life's longing for itself.
They come through you but not from you, and though they are with you, they do not belong to you.
You may house them but not their souls, for their souls dwell in the house of tomorrow, which you cannot even visit in your dreams."

His poem continues, but I think you will understand his message from these few lines.

MR. GREEN: I got you. This sounds very nice as a poem, but I don't think I would want the street to own my children. I trust my judgment better. I don't want my children to get their education from the terrible television shows, the magazines and the cheap movies.

DR. BAILEY: I am sure you'll agree that not all movies and all magazines are bad. Once in a while some very fine movies come out.

MR. GREEN: I agree, but I don't want my children to get a "once-in-a-while" education. Most of the movies are stupid and television shows are ridiculously bad. I have enough troubles making a livelihood. I don't need the additional heartache of seeing my children grow up under the influence of television.

DR. BAILEY: You have a point there.

MR. GREEN: Anyway... talking about troubles. Sometimes I wish God would exercise sometimes less equality in dishing out troubles to everyone. Some people can benefit by them more than others. I am surprised to see you with an expression of doubt on your face. You are a learned man. Don't you think I am right? I am talking from experience. Let me explain myself. There are people in this world who could benefit others—and maybe themselves too—by being saddled with some minor physical ailment.

DR. BAILEY (*With a mischievous smile of surprise on his face*): How is that?

MR. GREEN: Please, don't misunderstand me, professor. I don't wish disease on anybody, but I am sure you know there are people who cannot rest until they find ways to cause unhappiness to others. The better they feel, the more energy they use to hurt their fellow humans. I am sure that if they would be afflicted with some minor physical discomfort, something like constant sneezing or a perpetual itch—things of that sort—they would have less time to hurt others. As a matter of fact, my dear professor, those characters help me better understand why God had called for a day of rest after having created man (and woman). Sometimes, I wonder why God didn't call for a Sabbatical...

DR. BAILEY (*Breaking out in laughter*): There is sufficient reason for us to wonder about that!

MR. GREEN: You think I'm trying to be funny, professor. Actually, I am being serious, but a little humor doesn't harm. What should I do, cry? I have been struggling to understand God's mysterious reason for being so generous with giving the universe so much space, while He was so stingy in designing the character of man. I am sure he could have come up with a much better sample when He created man's character. God's choices, one must admit, defy human logic. Do you understand now, my dear professor, why God's works are such a mystery to me?

DR. BAILEY: Your fascination with heavenly matters is quite understandable. Perhaps a better version of the human species does exist if we begin looking at the human potential for good. There is something within us that exists aside from our bodies. Some refer to it as soul. That soul is our inner voice, which we rarely listen to. Children, I feel, are often more in touch with their inner souls, but when we grow up we forget its unique voice. I believe that if we could be more in touch with our inner selves, the world would change for the better. As far as justice is concerned, may I suggest to you, my friend, that God's justice or Heavenly justice, which I call Universal justice, does exist, and is real. It may not be necessarily in sync with man's concept of time, and may not be easily discernible to our limited human vision; but it nevertheless exists, even if not noticeable during the course of our lifetime.

MR. GREEN (*Nodding his head in partial agreement with the professor*): I think I know what you mean. I remember that the holy book tells us that God will remember the sins of fathers and their children to the third and fourth generation. That's all good and fine, but what I have in mind is that for us humans, life is too short. We like to see Heavenly justice take place before our own eyes, in our own lifetime.

DR. BAILEY: I guess we have to face the fact that no one asked our opinion on how the world should be created.

MR.GREEN: Talking about creation: my younger daughter is now learning in school about Darwin, so I read her book too. His idea is that human beings went through a long evolution before they became human. He claims that man started off like monkeys walking on four, and slowly learned to stand upright on two feet. Ha!

Big accomplishment! He calls it evolution. I wonder what gave him the bright idea that man evolved. He must have been kidding! What evolution?

DR. BAILEY (*Smiling*): Sometimes I wonder about that too.

MR. GREEN: How could Darwin call it evolution? That's ridiculous! I would give away my sewing machine if anyone could prove to me that people are better than monkeys. Since Adam and Eve were created, the history of mankind has been marching on with great pride under the illusion of progress, while adding to its pages mountains of stories of such stupidity, bestiality and barbarism and... what other word can be used, professor, to express this insanity?

DR. BAILEY: The Bible calls it sin.

MR. GREEN: You say sin? But, without having you thinking that I am arguing with the Bible, I feel that all the stuff that is happening around us is worse than sin. What I see is something different. What's that word, professor, I cannot think of it at the moment. What's that word I am looking for?

DR. BAILEY: I think I see your point. Sin is what we call a wicked act, but sin represents a kind of temporary departure from the laws of God; acts which seem more open to correction than the things we see happening in the world. Perhaps you mean regression?

MR. GREEN: Ah... Regression, you say? Yes, regression is what it should be called; moral regression under the cover of technical progress—a sort of regression that would, no doubt, cause profuse embarrassment to the dumbest ape. I want you to know that I have no intention to insult the ape world. It's just that we humans think so highly of ourselves and so little about apes that, by habit, we bring up the poor ape as an example of gross limitation.

(*He stops for a moment; looks like he is trying to recall the main theme of his discussion, and continues:*)

So, going back to evolution, the little I know of world history doesn't look to me like much progress. The first murder in the Bible—that of Cain killing his brother Abel—was out of jealousy.

By now, the repertoire of reasons for killing has multiplied by leaps and bounds: People use fancy names for killing each other. As the world "progressed," nations kill each other for "national pride." They pronounce their wars with great fanfare as "principles" that will save the world. Now we are even "blessed" with "holy" wars, encouraged—but, unfortunately not fought by—the so-called "holy" people themselves who instigate them. I wonder whether anybody who believes that man gradually managed to raise his body in the upright position and stand on two feet would think the effort was worth it. I suspect there would have been less killing if people had walked on four. Do you think that I am exaggerating, professor?

DR. BAILEY (*Smiling*): You may have a point there. Animals have more limited reasons for killing. But people who possess a more complex brain abuse it by trying to solve their problems with cleverness instead of intelligence, without paying attention to the fact that cleverness without intelligence equals stupidity.

MR. GREEN (*Nodding his head in surprise, indicating that he has recognized something he has not thought of before*):
I am beginning to realize that understanding does not necessarily go together automatically with knowledge. People can grow in knowledge while their understanding may not necessarily improve.

DR. BAILEY: One must also recognize that there are not many human beings that don't know the difference between good and bad. Doesn't your religion teach that man was given the choice between good and evil, life and death? Humanity has some responsibility for the kind of world it chooses to live in. People must not expect God to do their work.

MR. GREEN: Maybe man is not as smart as we think, because he makes wars with more ease than he makes peace. From my Bible studies, I can still remember a law that if you see a friend struggle with a fallen animal, you are supposed to help him. So if God asks us to help others, why can't we ask for a little help from Him when He sees us fall apart?

(*Waits, stops for a moment to see if Dr. Bailey has a comment, and continues*):

I have no serious answer to this, but I'll try a little humor. Imagine what life would be like if God would listen to a simple man like me, and overpopulate the world with saintly, righteous men (and women). Can you imagine what would happen? They would throw the whole world off balance. It could become a world of peace, a world without sins. Maybe this was not the Heavenly choice?

DR. BAILEY (*Laughingly*): I did not know that you were blessed with a sarcastic sense of humor, too, Mr. Green.

MR. GREEN: I don't know whether I am funny. My aunt Sarah, bless her, used to say: "If people want to have a better world, let them work for it." She was always on God's side. "Why should God send down ready-made saints and angels, and fill the world up with them? If I would be God, I would have done the same thing He is doing: keep all the good stuff he created—the angels and the saintly people—close to Him in heaven and let the people on earth fend for themselves. People got into the habit of acting like lazy beggars, asking God to do things for them they should be doing themselves. They are like panhandlers who have money in their pockets but go begging because they don't want to reach into their own pockets!" Furthermore, she added, "if God would have wanted to create a different world, He would have decided to make the Earth His permanent dwelling place, and send the devil to heaven."

In my humble opinion, it would not have been such a bad idea. We know, it is written somewhere that "the heavens belong to God and the earth was given to men." But, I swear to you, that not a soul would have minded if God had reversed things by making His permanent residence here on Earth, and placed the devil high enough over the Earth so he would get too dizzy to come down. I have no doubt that the devil himself would welcome the switch to a peaceful, restful residence in heaven, where he could live the life of a king—a life of leisure—instead of working with a busy schedule here on Earth. But then I realize that God has ideas we don't understand.

DR. BAILEY: I like your sense of humor, but I tend to side more with your Aunt Sarah. She seemed to have been not only on God's side but on mankind's side too. People cannot push civilization into an abyss of destruction and expect God to pull them out of it. People must not expect the consequences of thoughtlessness and insane actions to result in happiness, harmony and peace.

MR. GREEN (*In a questioning tone*): I wish I understood why God had to create insanity.

DR. BAILEY: Of course, if mankind's behavior had been programmed to be perfect, life would have been different. There would not even have been a need for the Ten Commandments. But we don't know why human nature is the way it is and we must accept what is. These laws exist because they are needed and it is within the power of mankind to live by them or not. May I also remind you, my friend, that your prophet Jeremiah said: "Out of the mouth of the Most High, proceeds neither evil nor good." I understand that to mean that God leaves the choice between good and evil up to man.

MR. GREEN: I understand what you are saying, professor, but I feel jittery having to rely on people to manage the world. I was taught to trust in God and I hope and pray He won't let me down; so my conclusion is: pray!

DR. BAILEY: I have some reservation about a generally accepted concept of prayer—the concept of supplication. Prayer, to me, constitutes the desire to lift one's consciousness and experience God's world on a higher level. It also is a form of expressing gratitude for what exists rather than of asking God to fix what man spoils. I assume you are familiar with the Jewish prayer in which man thanks God the first thing in the morning for returning his soul to him. I think it is a beautiful way of expressing appreciation of life. The crux of the matter is that a more profound appreciation of life leads to a greater love for all of creation and minimizes tendencies to hate and destroy.

MR. GREEN: Maybe prayers serve people on various levels? I know there are things in life to be grateful for, but there are problems that I don't feel capable of handling. Without God's guidance, I would feel lost. I would mind very much begging from people, but I don't mind pleading with God for his help.

DR. BAILEY: My friend, are you familiar with the Bible story about the flight of the Israelites from Egypt? The Bible says that when the Egyptian army was about to catch up with them as they were camping near the sea, the Israelites were frightened and complained to Moses. While Moses was trying to reassure them that God will fight for them, do you remember what God told Moses?

MR. GREEN: I am sorry, professor, but it has been too long a time since I studied the Bible, to remember details.

DR. BAILEY: According to the Bible, God said to Moses: "What for are you complaining to me? Tell the Israelites to move forward!" The lesson here is an obvious one. What would you do, my friend, if you could tell God directly your problems and God would tell you that you have to solve them yourself?

MR GREEN (*A little thrown off by the question, replies with some uncertainty in his voice*):
He did help in freeing them from slavery and suffering.
(*Glancing at his watch, Mr. Green looks surprised*):
I'd ask God if he considers me different than those people in the Bible. Oops... my watch tells me that my wife must be restless.

DR. BAILEY: You have certainly tried to cover a lot of ground for one morning, Mr. Green.

MR. GREEN: I am sorry, professor, but sometimes I get carried away with my thoughts and forget about my immediate troubles. When I think about my personal worries, I feel like anyone else in my shoes would—miserably poor. But when my thoughts take me into an excursion into the outside world and beyond into the heavens, I feel much better. The heavens above become my eternal palace, free of anguish and worry, while this Earth remains merely a short, temporary, wretched waiting room. Judging by my experience on Earth, the world beyond seems more promising. Maybe that's why my thoughts often wander off into the heavens.

Well, after all my jabber, I am still stuck with my troubles; but somehow, I feel better having talked to you, professor. Frankly, when I think of the world's problems, mine begin to look smaller. Yet, maybe I should go home and think of my own, earthly troubles. Every time I'm trying to get them out of my mind they keep coming back.

Mrs. Green walks on stage and finds Mr. Green.

MR. GREEN (*Looking startled*): My wife, you look restless. (*He gets up swiftly from the bench.*)

MRS. GREEN: You are still here, my husband? (*Turning to the professor*):
He is still talking? I bet he hasn't stopped talking to you since I left. He always talks about the heavens and the devil. I keep on telling him not to worry about the devil. He is well taken care of. God provided him with a full-time job. My husband is the one who could use a decent job.

MR. GREEN (*Interjects apologetically*): My wife says she has enough trouble thinking how to pay our rent. Who knows? Maybe the woman is right. Maybe God wants us to be busy putting our own houses in order and leave the divine order to His care?

Have yourself a nice day, professor. I hope you'll be able to find in your books some of the answers I am looking for. After all, a good education must be worth something! Am I right?

DR. BAILEY: I am not always so sure.

MR. GREEN: God bless you, professor.

DR. BAILEY: Same to you, my friend.

Mr. Green walks off the stage with his wife. Dr. Bailey continues reading. The lights on stage gradually dim.

PART 2
NONFICTION

Fragments from Childhood

Crib stories belong to mothers, and as much as these stories mean to them, they certainly cannot be considered choice reading material. But since they are my mother's snapshots of my early childhood, I beg forgiveness for making mention of them.

From the moment I was born, my mother said, I was a finicky child. I continued that behavior throughout my crib years and suspect that it lasted longer than that. My mother, having been a good soul, never complained to me about my baby years and childhood shenanigans, but she did tell me about them years after in her own good-natured way.

First of all, she said, I cried a lot when people used to stick their big heads into my crib, greeting me with baby talk. That sounds reasonable, don't you think? It is not easy to react favorably when people stick their noses and big faces into a crib while the baby lies helpless and feels claustrophobic before he or she even know what the word means. A baby is cornered and helpless, unable to run away. Whenever they did that—and they did it often—I cried inconsolably.

I also cried whenever my mother took me for strolls along the tree-lined streets of our hometown, Czernowitz. A violinist who apparently practiced a lot happened to live along the route. As soon as mother passed his window, I would start to cry all the way home. She must have felt quite despondent pushing a carriage with a child crying frantically. After a while she discovered the problem. She once stopped in front of the violinist's window, and, to her surprise I stopped crying. I listened until I fell asleep. Perhaps during those moments, I chose my profession... one that would both bring me much satisfaction as well as occasional butterflies in my stomach and a chance to learn humility.

Afternoons with God

By the time I reached the age of four, I had heard a lot about God and felt that being with Him could be quite exciting, but one had to be careful. Every afternoon, I would spend time with Him in our empty dining room, which served as a temporary prayer house for a small group of Hassidic followers and admirers of the Rebbe[1] from Mielnitza[2]. The room was dark. Its only window faced the courtyard and never received direct sunlight. But it was quiet and peaceful, and the perpetual click of the ticking alarm clock on top of the table helped to accentuate that silence. It became my favorite room in the afternoons.

"God is here," I thought to myself, "and he must be waiting for the people to arrive for their prayers." I knew very well where God was! He was lurking from behind the velvet covering of the ark where the Torah[3] scrolls were resting. I cannot recall exactly the source of my information, but I must have heard it from the older boys who had started Heder[4] before me.

---

1 In this context, Hassidic Rabbi.
2 The name of a small town or Shtetl in what was once Poland, now Ukraine.
3 Scrolls containing the Five Books of Moses—Pentateuch.
4 Religious school. Literal translation: room.

It felt good being with God, especially since I was under the table and the table was quite sturdy. It isn't that I didn't trust God; everybody said He could be trusted. But what if He happens to be in a bad mood? I heard that sometimes He could get quite angry. Therefore, the table, aside from being a comfortable canopy, also served as a protective shelter... just in case...

The clock and I became good friends, and I soon discovered that it sounded happy on sunny days and a little sad on rainy days. However, most of the time it was a happy clock and we would often be ticking time cheerfully together. I was quite certain that the clock had as much pleasure being there as I did. It also felt reassuring that the clock stood on the table over me, the reasons being, firstly, if God wanted to come out and talk to us, the clock over me would be the first to meet Him. That made me feel much more comfortable. I am shy with strangers, and I hadn't met Him yet. Secondly, if God was in a bad mood, I knew that the clock, being much older and knowing God for a long time, would know better than I how to talk to Him. I knew that the clock had a special language. But since God knew all languages, there would be no problem; they could talk to each other. I wanted first to find out in what mood God was before I met him.

My afternoons alone with God and the clock were interrupted as soon as the first people arrived for the prayers. Then the room became alive with the sounds of Psalm recitations, mingled with lively discussions on some Talmudic question or the latest events of the day. Once the service started, all those voices suddenly molded into the Psalm of Ashrei—"Happy are those who dwell in Thy house"—and the afternoon service began.

As I reached my fourth birthday, my quiet, peaceful afternoons had to finally come to an end. I was now fit for religious studies, and the time came for me to begin finding God in the holy books.

One afternoon before the services, Father called me from under the table and asked me if I would like to begin attending Heder. Sensing that my father, whom I loved very much, would have liked me to say yes, and also due to a certain measure of curiosity about joining an activity reserved for older boys, I smiled and nodded my head for yes. After seeing my father's face light up with a big smile, I felt that my answer was the right one.

One week later, I overheard my father asking the melamed[5] :

"Do you think the boy should be starting Heder? He is a little small, isn't he?"

"Well," said the melamed, looking me over with a pitiful grimace on his face and stroking his beard thoughtfully, "He is a little small for his age, but it won't harm him to get an early start."

Several days after the conversation with the melamed, Father brought me to the Heder. I was glad he came with me, especially since I started having doubts whether I really wanted to start Heder.

When we arrived, the melamed welcomed me with an affectionate but painful pinch on my left cheek. I suddenly had the desire to let out a scream, but had to subdue myself because of the presence of the other boys. While I was recovering from that unexpected welcome, I was shown to an empty space on the bench and my studies began.

The melamed, whom we called "rebbe" in class, looked ancient. His head made a strong impression on me. It was big, round and bald, covered with a huge yarmulke. "The moon must look like that when it wears a skullcap," I thought to myself. His overgrown, silver-gray beard and large mustache covered most of his face, and it was difficult to see his features.

"Wow, what a big beard," I thought with awe. "I bet he has to water it every morning."

His large, blue eyes were always dancing and were partially eclipsed by thick, long, gray eyebrows, which he frequently, almost automatically, raised when confronted with a question. His favorite teaching tool was a yellow pointer, consisting of a converted toothbrush handle, which he treated with guarded care and tenderness as if it were a rare diamond. That pointer turned out to be indispensable in helping us sort out the Hebrew letters we were learning. On top of the long table, along scattered books of various sizes, stood an old, worn-out kerosene lamp that looked like it had been used by the melamed's grandfather's grandfather. Its faint, dancing flicker was more of a distraction than help in our reading. (Electricity was too expensive in those days.) Next to the lamp, I

---

5 Teacher of basic religious studies.

spotted a wooden rod—a kantchik[6]—as we referred to it with no small amount of reverence. I remembered having seen carriage drivers passing by our street use similar sticks for their horses.

"Maybe," I thought to myself, "the melamed has horses too?"

However, my guess soon proved wrong. The only horses our rebbe[7] could afford were his "little horses," a name designated for us and often interchanged with sheidim—devils. As it turned out, the kantchik was sort of a training tool that served as a deterrent against excessive rambunctious behavior. It even helped us sometimes (but not always), in redirecting our minds to the studies.

Our Heder's large window faced a courtyard, which served as a thoroughfare, connecting two streets. Several large, majestic trees adorned the courtyard and attracted considerable birds, and animal activity. Unfortunately, the rebbe had a difficult time competing with the hustle and bustle outside, which consistently challenged our ability to concentrate on our studies and jeopardized his chances of holding our attention. It therefore became necessary for him to perform that magic act of dissipating noise in the Heder with his celebrated wand. But, a strange thing happened; the more the rod came into use, the more we became experts on the various activities out in the courtyard.

First, a stocky little man passed by daily at three o'clock in the afternoons with his shopping bag. His walk was especially interesting to us. There was a curious bounce to his walk, and to us it appeared like he was practicing daily bandy-legged dancing. We all watched his movements carefully, swaying our bodies in unison with him, trying to become the best at mimicking his movements. At the end of the week, a bandy-legged-style dance-walk contest was organized and we danced our way home. The winner became the recipient of a coveted prize—a seat closest to the Heder window the next day. Shaye, the oldest in the class, was both organizer and juror. His final judgment was indisputable and his high standards beyond reproach. There were two main reasons for the high regard he commanded: One, a very important one: he was one year older; and the other—certainly not of lesser value—were his pants. He was the only fellow in class who wore long pants. True, they were short for his size, but nevertheless, they were long, and that's what really counted.

6 Rod.
7 Another term for teacher, interchangeable with melamed.

In addition to the bandy-legged dancing walker, we were equally fascinated by a black-and-white cat and its four vivacious kittens. Two of them were completely black, while the others had white paws. There was no question in our minds that the kittens had chosen to have their meals and playing sessions in front of our window being fully aware that a loyal, most admiring audience was watching them intently from inside through the big window. Their presence alone was enough to get our undivided attention.

In addition, birds of all kinds came to visit us, landing gracefully on the window ledge, waiting for food, which we gladly provided during our recess. We made up names for them according to their color and size. Those who were not distinguishable in size received the same name. The birds commanded our greatest respect. After all, can you imagine being able to fly? And with such ease! Whenever they felt like flying all they did was lift their tiny wings and off they went into the sky! That takes brains! Not even our rebbe could do that!

There was so much to see! Who could resist all that activity?

There were certain days that added to our restlessness and were not helpful to the rebbe in keeping us focused on our studies.

The most welcomed schooldays were the ones preceding a holiday, and, of course, Friday—the last and shortest day of our study week. We arrived at one o'clock and knew that in one hour we would be free from the confines of the Heder and on our way home, exempt from study for two full days. What's more, there were delicious, crunchy potato pancakes waiting at home. These were not just potato pancakes. They simply melted in your mouth. What a wonderful time to look forward to!

However, good days can have sometimes their downside too. Saturday, a day that we looked forward to with great excitement and anticipation, happened also to be a day during which fathers had time to query their children about their studies. That presented an awkward situation. I knew that the activities I watched through the window were not exactly what Father had in mind. How could I tell him about the cat and the cute kittens, the bandy-legged dancer, or the birds on the window ledge?

I knew I had a problem and felt that the table in our dark dining-prayer-room was the perfect solution to my predicament. For several

Sabbaths, after lunch, when father usually had some time to himself, I sneaked into the prayer room and disappeared under the table.

The room was dark and peaceful, as usual, and the clock faithfully continued its monotonous, happy tick. God was, as usual, inside the ark, but resting, of course (since it was Sabbath), and so was I—under the table. However, after practicing invisibility for several Sabbaths in a row, my father's curiosity led him to my secret, peaceful abode. I had finally been discovered.

"What are you doing under the table?" Father wanted to know.

"Well... hm... I am resting..."

There was no way out. Hesitatingly I had to crawl out from under and sit down with Father at the table. I dreaded the questions awaiting me, but there was no way out. I had to divulge my week's experiences. I gave him a full report and detailed description of the cat and the kittens, the bandy-legged dancer and the birds on the window ledge, and expected a harsh reprimand. My restlessness grew by the second. Having finished my account, I avoided looking at Father for fear of making things worse. "Who knows," my mind whispered in fear, "how many spanks I will be getting for this? Will father do that? He never spanked me before. But this time it looks like I will be getting it!"

Finally, I dared lifting my head. With a sheepish, guilty glance, I looked at father timidly, awaiting his verdict. To my surprise, a bright, mischievous smile appeared on his face. Is it possible that he remembered his own childhood days?

Be it as it may, the smile on Father's face gave me confidence to go back to Heder the next Monday.

Heder and School, An Unexpected Education
(Angels, Devils and Ghosts)

When the time came to begin public school, there were some unexpected surprises. These were more along the lines of what we would now call "life lessons."

One such lesson took place on home ground, on a street in my hometown, Czernovitz[8]. I remember the street vividly. It was named Hauptstrasse—main street in German. (Although our area was under Romanian rule up until the Second World War, the German

---

8 *This city is now called Chernivtsi and is part of the Ukraine.*

language was still in use and dated back to the time when our area was still a part of the Hungarian Austrian Empire.)

The first lesson took place on my first day on the way to grade school. It was on a bright, sunny autumn day. Our city was built on a hill and its streetcars would make ascending sounds as they struggled their way upward. Having already started music lessons, I would sing along with the cars, making up imaginary chromatic scales.

"You, dirty Jew—you Jesus killer," a boy with a schoolbag on his back yelled at me and ran off on his way to school. He seemed a year or two older and was well dressed. He looked like he was ahead of me in certain areas of knowledge.

"Why did he call me 'dirty Jew,'" I asked Father after returning from school, "and who is Jesus? And why did he call me Jesus killer?" I was quite upset and couldn't understand why the boy yelled at me. I had never heard that kind of talk before, but then, I had never before walked on the Hauptstrasse early in the morning when children go to school.

"Don't pay attention to such things. When you get older, you'll understand."

Father was half right. I did get older.

As a result of several similar experiences, my elementary school years were not quite jolly.

It was a relief coming from school and entering the Heder. School hours were from nine in the morning until one in the afternoon, and Heder hours started two hours later. Heder felt safe. In time, I even began to be grateful for spending afternoons there. We were able to ask questions, even if we didn't always get answers. The winter days were freezing but it felt comfortable knowing we were close to home.

The Second Year of Heder:
Spending a Day With Angels and the Flood

It was on a bitter cold day. There were eight of us children huddled together around a large wooden table. The room was small with bare, yellowing white walls. We would have preferred being home on an afternoon like that, especially after having to spend the morning in school. But at least, we were in a warm room. It was pleasant watching the glittering coal simmering inside the big wall-oven, with its cozy, warm air flowing towards us.

The table was crowded with holy books of various sizes, and in the center rested a giant-sized book with heavy, tattered leather covers. We starred at it with awe mingled with fear. It was a Talmud, and its presence served as a reminder that our studies were not going to become easier.

The rebbe noticed our uneasiness at the sight of that huge book and watched us with probing eyes.

"Don't worry," he reassured us, "you will not have to study from it for a while."

"How about next year?"

"Next year is another year."

He took off his jacket and rolled up his sleeves like a hard laborer about to begin lifting heavy weights. Hesitantly, as if he was already tired before even starting, the rebbe picked up a faded, brown leaderbound Humash[9] from the table. Its sagging covers and brittle pages looked as if they could disintegrate upon touch. They bore witness to constant use by hundreds of children's hands pawing through its tired pages. With his head slightly bent and his glasses perched on the tip of his nose, he glanced at us through his eyeglasses with his penetrating blue eyes. A short grin on his face quickly changed into a more serious expression, and once he began clearing his throat we knew the class was about to begin.

Sitting on two wobbly, squeaky wooden benches opposite each other, we picked up the book of Genesis waiting for us on the table. As we read the stories of Adam and Eve in the Garden of Eden, we were open-mouthed with curiosity. What better place could there be than the Garden of Eden? I saw myself walking with my friends in beautiful gardens. Nobody throws stones there! No snowstorms, no school, no tests; no need to ask Father for money to buy sweets. I could eat all the chocolate and ice cream I wanted. So what if God doesn't want us to eat from the fruit tree in the middle of the Garden. That wouldn't bother me at all! I don't like fruit anyway.

We couldn't understand why God didn't allow Adam and Eve to eat from that tree. "If He didn't want them to eat the fruit, why did

9 Pentateuch—*The Five books of Moses.*

He plant it in the first place?" we asked.

"God tested them," the rebbe said

"So they were tested too, just like us?"

"Not quite."

"Grownups get different tests?"

"Yes," the rebbe smiled.

"Every Friday?"

"Whenever God wants."

We were not happy with the rebbe's answer. God is not like the rebbe! He can make people know everything without teaching them, so what are the tests for?

The rebbe should really know more about these tests. We were disappointed. The rebbe noticed our dissatisfaction with his answers and continued reading for us the story about the serpent talking Eve into eating the forbidden fruit.

"What kind of a serpent was that, a serpent that talks? They showed us in school a serpent. It couldn't say a single word! Dogs and cats can talk; but serpents?"

Then we heard the story of the one that killed his brother. (Was it Cain that killed Hevel[10], or the other way around?) For some reason, we confused their names; perhaps because we didn't like the story.

"Why did God ask Cain where Hevel was? Doesn't God know everything?"

Our teacher became impatient and brushed us off: "If you want to know the answers to these questions, you'll have to wait until you get older and study the commentaries."

Another story we didn't like was the one about the flood and the whole world drowning in deep waters; that was scary, very scary! There were some bad people in our city. They could make God angry and make Him send another flood. We did find out that God promised not to make more floods. But what if He changes his mind?

This story kept haunting me for a long time, especially in the fall when the winds began making angry sounds as they were beating the rain-soaked leaves, tearing them cruelly off their branches. On such days I could see our city flooding and the houses going under. Of course, our apartment house and those of other nice people

---

10 Hebrew for Abel.

would be saved and float upon the deep waters just like Noah's ark. In addition, we lived on the floor above the rabbi of Mielnitza, a very holy man, so we were completely safe. On the other hand, it might be a good idea to ask mother to teach my sister Eva and I to swim. You never know when it might come in handy...

Both Eva and I were frightened of water. I don't remember exactly what triggered Eva's fear, but my anxiety of water started even before I learned about Noah and the flood. It was during a hot summer day when I made my first acquaintance with water. Mother took us to the Prut river on the outskirts of our hometown, Czernowitz. I loved standing on the edge of the river watching the pebbles through the clear, transparent water. It was lots of fun until mother decided to take us further into the water for a dip. I did not exactly come out a winner of that experience. After I swallowed more water than my body was willing to tolerate, I was convinced that repeating this experience would not be in my favor. Needless to say, after learning about the flood, my attitude to water did not improve.

Most of my friends did not share my fear of water. I would watch them swim like fish when we were together at the river. But I was not jealous. I was quite satisfied watching them.

However, all the boys in class shared one fear. It made us feel even more restless than the story of the flood; and that was being questioned by the rebbe at the end of the week. He was strict and demanding of us. He wanted us to remember everything we studied! Everything! He kept warning us during class: "You better pay attention, or else your parents will find out about it!"

Trying to avoid more interruptions with questions, the rebbe decided to read for us another story. A narrow beam of pale, wintry sunlight made short visits on the dimly lit table, appearing and disappearing in a teasing game of hide and seek. Amidst the chatter of our high-pitched voices, he turned the pages to the story of Abraham, the three guests and the hospitality he offered them, inviting them into his tent and treating them to food and drink. He called out the page number and in chanting tones motioned us to join him. Our heads and bodies began swaying back and forth, and we followed him in unison with feigned enthusiasm.

"God appeared to him (Abraham)... as he sat at the tent door in the heat of the day; and he raised his eyes and saw three men standing near him; and when he saw them, he ran from the door of the tent to meet them, and bowed himself to the ground..."

The rebbe interrupted his reading. He looked at us intently and spoke softly. Whenever he spoke in that tone of voice, we knew that a big secret was about to be revealed.

"These three men," he told us in a tone of confidentiality, "were the angels Michael, Gabriel and Raphael—they were not people of flesh and blood. They were real angels posing as regular human beings—r e a l a n g e l s !" He emphasized his words with great care, and whenever he did that, his big, uneven teeth would protrude and distract me. But this time the thought of angels was enough to make me forget the rebbe's teeth. I was carried away by the image of angels, and so was the rest of the class. Our casual jabber, which usually accompanied the rebbe's reading, suddenly abated. As if a steam locomotive engine had come to a grinding halt, our almost mechanical head-and-body swaying came to a complete standstill. Somewhat like the deceiving calm before a storm, a brief moment of hushed silence took over the room, and soon with an outburst of enthusiastic gestures we began showering the beleaguered rebbe with questions:

"Rebbe," Fayvl the Frog raised his voice from across the table, bouncing with excitement. "Rebbe, how do angels look? Do they really have wings, like my brother says?"

Anxious to be noticed by the rebbe, he kneeled on the bench in order to raise his body a little higher, while lifting his hand and waving it wildly to get the rebbe's attention.

"Rebbe, please tell me. Do they also have to go to Heder when they are small?"

Fayvl the Frog was the youngest in our group, and small enough to merit that pet name with honors. It stuck to him like a bee to honey. One could not say the name Fayvl without adding his nickname to it. Fayvl's favorite activities were crawling and/or jumping. Regular walking was not part of his repertoire. He never entered the Heder with normal steps; he hopped his way in, and during breaks in the spring time, when the soil became warm enough for crawling, he could be found with his head close to the ground, watching insects.

"Rebbe, Rebbe," asked another, "Is it true that there are also bad angels? Is it true?"

"Rebbe, please, please, can angels get sick? Do they also get the mumps?"

Our rebbe took off his metal-rimmed glasses, ripped a piece of newspaper resting on the nearby bookstand, and began cleaning them nervously. His chunky fingers moved restlessly with short, swift motions over the glass. Gazing meditatively into the distance, as if answering questions to himself, he turned to us in a low voice:

"Children," he said, "it is true that the Torah speaks to us in human language, but it is also written that 'The Heaven belongs to God and the Earth was given to people.'"

"Anybody knows what this means, children?" No one answered.

"Anybody?" the rebbe repeated... There was silence. It was a tough question and no one even dared to guess an answer.

"It means, children, that we must not stick our noses where they don't belong! Do you understand?"

Suddenly, raising his voice, the Rebbe straightened out his body with a swift motion as if woken up from a dream.

"Now, children, let's not waste more time. We must go on; I don't want you to act like potato heads when your fathers ask you what you learned."

The rebbe put his glasses back on and continued:

"And Abraham said..."

Somehow, my attention began to falter. I found myself unable to follow the reading. My mind became preoccupied with the idea of visiting angels. I started daydreaming and my scenery changed completely. My thoughts took me back home to our apartment...

It is Friday night. The table in the dining area of our kitchen is covered with a white tablecloth. In the customary Sabbath manner, a bottle of wine stands ready for the Kiddush[11] and the soft, cheerful candlelight adds a special, festive, warm atmosphere. Father returns from the Evening Service at the synagogue and begins to recite "Sholem Aleichem[12]"—a hymn welcoming the angels. No sooner does he finish singing that something unbelievable happens. Can it be true? Three men appear at our kitchen door. I knew immediately

---

11 Blessing for the wine.
12 According to tradition, an angel accompanies each person after the services home on Friday night.

that these were not ordinary people. Their presence is both mysterious and pleasing. Something unusual is happening. I see their faces but cannot tell how they actually look. They appear neither young nor old. In spite of straining my eyes to see how they are dressed, all I can see is three men. Strange! Very strange! Squinting through the candlelight, I notice a halo over the heads of everyone sitting at the table. Maybe it's the same halo the older boys talked about—the one that rested on Moses' head? Or, maybe the guests put a halo on everyone's head at the table without even my noticing it? Who knows? But one thing is for sure: These visitors are not people; they are real angels! Father notices them, and I can tell from the gleeful look on his face that he knows who these unexpected guests are. In honor of this unusual occasion he decides to omit "Tzeitchem L'Shalom.[13]" He invites them to join us at the table, and they gladly consent. Hastily, room is made for them and Father makes the blessing over the wine. His face shines with pride and happiness at the honor of such important visitors. After all, what greater honor can there be than having angel visitors at the Sabbath table! Mother is busy serving the meal and our guests delight in her cooking. Father is watching me and notices that I am not eating.

"Why don't you eat? You'll be hungry later. What are you trying to do, fast?"

But who can eat with all this happening? I keep looking at our visitors and cannot take my eyes away from them.

For all I know, two of these angels may be the famous Michael and Gabriel! Wouldn't that be something? Is it possible that they are actually sitting at our table? These are not just angels. They are the most important angels. They sit up in Heaven next to God Himself! The rebbe told us about it! Michael sits to God's right and Gabriel, to His left! And who is the third one? He must be their assistant, a terribly important angel for sure! What a treat! I can't believe this is happening! I bet they must know more about God than anybody else in the whole world.

All I have to do now is be patient and wait for the meal to end and I'll be able to ask them questions. They are right here at the table, and they are so nice! They won't mind if I ask them a couple

---

13 *Bidding the angels: "Leave in Peace."*

of questions. I guess I'll first have to convince Father to let me talk to them. I know he doesn't like me to bother guests with questions, especially such distinguished guests. "Don't bother people with questions," he always tells me. But if worse comes to worse, I'm sure he will let me ask them at least one question.

I asked Father many times what God is like and he never gave me an answer. The angels are so nice! I'm sure they won't mind if I asked them just that one question. They will be able to tell me. After all, they sit next to him. I hear so many different stories about God. At times he is very nice, and other times they say He gets angry very fast. Now I'll find out the real truth. And tomorrow morning when I'll see the boys in Shul[14] I can't wait to watch their faces when I tell them what happened. Will they be surprised!

A slight poke on my shoulder suddenly interrupted my reveries. It was the rebbe trying to get my attention.

"Hey, little fellow, this is no time for daydreaming. Come on, let's get to work! Start reading!" The rebbe noticed that I lost my place in the book because I started turning pages back and forth. He had a surprised look on his face, but must have decided to ignore my missed part of the reading. "Come on, read! We have very little time left!"

"And two angels came to Sodom in the evening, and Lot sat at the gate of Sodom, and Lot, seeing them, rose up to meet them..."

I kept on reading and was shocked to find out that the people of Sodom wanted to kill Lot because he was nice to strangers. Terrible people! I wished the rebbe had not taken me away from the visiting angels.

But now I understood angels better. I knew why they came down from heaven. They came because they were needed. They were no more strange creatures hidden somewhere in heaven. I saw them with my own eyes! Just as they came down and saved Lot, they would show up again anytime people are in trouble; even if a flood came ever again.

A sense of relief came over me. There was nothing to worry about anymore.

The sun began its setting journey in the sky and its narrow beam inside our room hastily retreated into a corner, leaving our table in

14 Synagogue.

semi-darkness, bidding us meekly goodbye. The bouncing flame of the dimming oil-lamp started struggling with its last gasps.

The rebbe took off his glasses. He looked worn out, but he had a broad smile on his face. With an affectionate twinkle in his eyes and an obvious sigh of relief, he said:

"That's it, children; time to go home. Dear God!" he said, lifting his hands toward heaven. "You keep on sending me little devils every year. How about a few angels for a change?"

The Heder (school) that the author attended as a child in Czernowitz.

*Family photograph taken in 1936, when Sam Marder (standing in front) was six years old.
Also pictured from left to right: Dvorah (aunt), Eva (sister), Berl (father) and Esther (mother).*

Herr Schwartz

I must have been about six years old when I first saw Herr Schwartz at Father's grocery store. After Father came home in the evening, I asked him, "Dad, who was that man this afternoon in the store?"

"He is a friend," Father said.

"I like him," I said, "but he is so quiet! He hardly talks!"

"He has more to say than many people who talk a lot," Father said with an affectionate laugh.

Herr Schwartz was German. He seemed older than Father. Father's friendship with Herr Schwartz dated back to several years before I was born (so my father told me). Although I knew nothing of him, I liked him at first sight. Almost daily, returning from school in the afternoons, I would find Herr Schwartz in the store. He was always dressed in a three-piece gray suit—it must have been his favorite color—and a bow tie. He knew when to come to Father's store. He chose afternoons after most housewives had done their grocery shopping. He would just walk in to the store, greet Father, sit and keep him company. I don't remember him ever engaging in conversations with strangers. He was silent even in the presence of children. Whenever my friends and I would stop by at the store and greet him, he usually responded with a slight nod and mild smile. He did not fuss with us kids as other people did; yet I felt he liked us. His gentle, serene look made me feel good in his presence, and that feeling continued throughout the few years I was privileged to see him during his visits with Father.

I remember him always relaxed, sitting on a stool with his legs crossed, as if it was the most comfortable lounge. Father's store was so small that when two customers came in it made me feel cramped. I had to get out into the street. But Herr Schwartz sat calmly. He seemed to project not only a presence of "gemuttlichkeit," an aura of comfort—that charming characteristic of old-time Austria prevalent in our hometown in those days—but also a feeling of peace.

Father and Herr Schwartz had no business relationships, and I wondered what led to their friendship. After I started school, I became aware of the anti-Semitic atmosphere in which we lived and realized that relationships such as those between Herr Schwartz and Father were rare.

It made me feel good to see their friendship continue, untouched by the poisoned currents of ethnic animosities which were increasing in our city and, generally, throughout Romania. As I got older, I came to understand that what my father and Herr Schwartz shared was a strong bond based on their unfailing faith in people, and their profound concern for mankind, which extended itself beyond their respective immediate cultural and religious communities.

As the Second World War came closer, political instability and social unrest in Romania were on the rise and, as is usually the case in such times, fear of violence against Jews increased. During a short period of fascist rule, looting, beatings and shootings were the order of the day. In 1938, like all Jewish people in Romania, Father lost his citizenship and the general atmosphere grew tenser with each day. I remember Herr Schwartz warning Father:

"The political situation is deteriorating. See if you and the family can find some way to get out of here. I see bad times ahead if a war breaks out," Herr Schwartz said. "There is news coming from Vienna of Jews being shot in their homes and on the streets. I would have never believed that this could ever happen in a city like Vienna!"

"I don't think these horrible incidents will continue," Father said. "Austria and Germany are countries of culture and will never fall for the Nazi ideology. Besides, the world would never tolerate Hitler's insane plans. Even if we wanted to leave now, there is no place we can go. My wife's brother in America works in a factory and I don't think he has the money to make out immigration papers for us."

When the Soviet Union annexed the areas of Bucovina and Bessarabia in 1940, new problems arose. The new government brandished all merchants as "enemies of the Proletariat." Even small storekeepers like my father were considered "capitalists." To avoid the dangers of being classified as such (in most cases it resulted in deportation), Father gave up his store and took on a position as bookkeeper and night watchman. He did it with a sense of relief because the store had been a financial burden to him throughout the years. Besides, by becoming a "workman," his social status changed from the undesirable label of "businessman" to "worker." His new job also offered him the opportunity to be off on the Sabbath.

During those early first weeks of the Soviet Regime, when Father still had the store, Herr Schwartz continued visiting him. Since it was summertime, I was off from school and spent more time with Father at the store listening to his conversations with Herr Schwartz.

"What do you think, Herr Marder, will be the outcome of the pact between Stalin and Hitler," I remember Herr Schwartz asking Father.

"I doubt whether either one of them is taking the other seriously," Father said. "I don't trust dictators, especially these two. Eventually they will want to swallow each other up."

This kind of a discussion in Stalin's Russia was a rarity because only highly trusted friends dared to discuss openly their political views. Saying something of a negative nature about "Little Father Stalin" was enough to result in your arrest and eventual disappearance.

With the passing of time, the Soviet regime's incarcerations and deportations to Siberia intensified and people lived in constant fear. No family knew if they might be next. It became a matter of routine to be awakened at night by the roar of Soviet secret-police trucks arriving to pick up families from their homes, never to be seen or heard of again. Neighbors huddled together, relating the latest news to each other by whisper, fearing to be overheard.

Little did people realize then, that some of those deportees were unintentionally being saved. Ironically, the Siberian labor camps, as bad as they were, indirectly saved their lives. Had they been left in their homes by the Soviet authorities, they would have been transported a year later by the Nazis to Transnistria,[1] where a majority of people ended up in mass graves. No one expected a Nazi invasion and the oncoming of a Holocaust. Being in Siberia, the deportees were out of touch with the rest of the world and were not even aware of the existence of Nazi death camps until after the war. Of course, not all those sent to Siberia survived the conditions there, but many, more would have died had they been in Transnistria.

During that period, Father maintained some contact with Herr Schwartz, but their meetings were less frequent. To this day I don't know why.

In the summer of 1941, when Hitler's armies entered Austria, and news about atrocities against Jews and mass-murder reached us from Vienna, Father did not trust their veracity. He thought the news was fabricated by Communist propaganda. Although we were familiar with Hitler's ranting speeches on the radio about the annihilation of Jews, Father and others did not give up their optimism.

Some people, however, felt danger coming and made attempts to flee to other continents, but far too few countries were ready to admit them.

The Nazis Enter Czernowitz

When the Nazis marched into town, an eerie silence and intense fear overtook the city. People stayed inside their homes and no one ventured out into the streets. The arrival of the German Nazi troops and their allied Romanian soldiers started a period of horror and

---

1 *An area of the Ukraine which was handed over by the Nazis to Romania , and where concentration camps were established for Jews from Bucovina and Bessarabia.*

atrocities. Tragedy came closer to home. Three thousand Jews were rounded up and killed and hundreds of homes were plundered during the course of several days. The Temple, one of the most beautiful houses of prayer in that part of the world, was set on fire and community leaders, along with 150 other men, were marched to the river Prut on the outskirts of the city and shot. These executions by the Nazi and Romanian soldiers were aided by local Ukrainian, Ruthenian and Romanian gangs. Despite the horrors, Father still felt that those murders were committed by gangs and undisciplined armies.

However, an early decree issued by the Nazis in July 1941, made people realize the new rules were part of an official policy:

Decree Nr. 1344, July 30, 1941

In the interest of public safety and security, we, Alexander Riosanu, as authorized by Mr. General Ion Antonescu for the administration of Bucovina, hereby proclaim that:

Street traffic for groups of more than three Jews is strictly forbidden, and can only take place between the hours of 16-20...

Jews are allowed to shop in the marketplaces only between the hours of 9:30-11. Bread can only be bought after 6 o'clock...

Jews who have practices in self-employed professions must immediately put up a sign at the entrance of their offices "Jew" along with their name, profession and hours of practice...

Jews of all ages and both sexes are required to wear prominently, as a sign of recognition, on the left side of their chests, a yellow star, made up of two, even, three-cornered pieces of linen, to form a Jewish star, measuring six centimeters from its center. Any digression from these laws will be punishable with camp internment or more stringent measures as applicable by law.

Alexander Riosanu

"Stringent measures" meant that for "disturbing the order," every tenth Jew would be shot. A segment of the Jewish population still preferred to believe that the decree was a passing evil that will eventually change in time.

In October of that year, a Ghetto was established in Czernowitz. The Ghetto was separated from the outside world with barbed wire and guarded by armed soldiers. Those who had apartments in areas outside the Ghetto limits were ordered to evacuate their premises by six o'clock that evening or be shot. No one was permitted to leave the enclosed area. Because our street (Eminescu) was included in the Ghetto zone, Father and Mother were able to take in other families who were expelled from their homes outside the designated area. Optimistic rumors were still circulating that the Ghetto would not last long and people continued to harbor hope that "things will change." Another rumor had it that we would eventually be taken out of the Ghetto and be sent away to do work in the fields.

On an early morning the same month, we woke up to a commotion outside. Looking out the window, we saw soldiers on our street. From the nearby buildings people came out carrying valises and knapsacks on their backs. They placed their baggage at the center of the street and were lining up. The street was filled with sounds of crying babies mixed with calls of parents searching for their children in the crowd. Before anyone in our apartment had a chance to go down into the street to find out what was happening, a soldier appeared at our door and told us that we were being "evacuated." We were ordered to go out into the street to be marched to the train station. The apartments would later be searched, and anyone found in them would be shot. The soldier seemed to have some sympathy because he broke the news to us in a mild manner:

"Pack up all the food and clothing you can," he said, "because no one knows where you will be going."

Decisions had to be made in a manner of minutes on what food and other necessities to take along this terrifying journey to an unknown destination.

I watched Father as he quickly and nervously packed essential belongings. He was quiet. His face, which always projected optimism and hope, even when faced with difficult problems, now looked drawn and in a state of disbelief.

Amidst all the rush and confusion and the frantic packing, we heard knocking on the door. It was a surprise we certainly did not expect: Herr Schwartz. How he entered the Ghetto and whether he entered it legally, we didn't know; but it really didn't matter, because what he had intended to do was by far more dangerous than entering the Ghetto.

"We have no time," Herr Schwartz said to Father with urgency. "Gather some belongings quickly and come with me. I have a way of getting you and the family out of the Ghetto. I will take care of you for as long as will be necessary."

Father was touched: "My dear Herr Schwartz, we cannot stay while others are going. If everyone goes, we have to go too." Father thanked him for his kindness. Herr Schwartz tried to convince Father that we must not join the convoy:

"You can see, Herr Marder, that this is a matter of life and death. No one knows where you and your family will be sent. The only solution is not to go. The war will not last forever."

There was no time for long discussions. Father's mind was made up, and Herr Schwartz left sad and disappointed.

We immediately began to carry our frantically packed sacks downstairs. Father made sure to lock our apartment door "in case they might change their orders" and send us back home. "You never know," he said, still maintaining optimism. We even made sure that our cat would have some food outside the door "until we return." Three-and-a-half years later, after we returned, we were told that the poor animal was sitting in front of our door for weeks, waiting for our door to open.

•   •   •

During those endless days, weeks, months and years in Transnistria, Father's untimely death was the greatest emotional blow. Herr Schwartz's warnings to Father kept haunting me. If Father had only listened to his friend, he would have been alive, I kept saying to myself. As far as our existence was concerned, there were ironically only a few days during which we had assurance we would not be killed. Some German soldiers stationed nearby in that area for a few weeks told us that "at the moment" there were no orders to kill us. But most of our existence during those years was surrounded by the daily mystery of when our lives would end. The conflict between a sense of futility, the value of staying alive in an insane world, and a faintly kindled struggle to survive the starvation, hopelessness and despair, made me think of Herr Schwartz. His special kindness made me feel that good people also existed. That dampened to some extent my feelings of hopelessness. But generally, those years did not give any room for supporting the thought of ever getting out and returning home. Living daily on a razor-edge line between life and death does not allow much for daydreaming. The fight to survive from day to day takes precedence over all dreams and hopes. It is only during special moments that a daring thought from somewhere deep within, about a life devoid of starvation, interrupted sometime the daily routine and the image of imminent death looming.

However, after years that felt like an eternity, the unbelievable happened. The war began coming to a close and the Soviet army finally freed us. After the liberation from those camps, my mother, sister, our cousin Aaron, and I did manage, albeit with great difficulty, to return home to Czernowitz. Because the Nazis took away our documents, we had to return as nonexistent entities. (Ironically, those who cooperated with the Nazis lived in comfort after the Soviets returned to our home city. These were people who plundered the homes of those who were deported to Transnistria.)

We knew that the conditions for us to stay and live normal lives were hopeless, because when we were finally issued documents, they were temporary ones. This was ample proof in those days that we could be sent away anytime into undesirable areas of Russia for forced labor. We were not ready for a new period of misery and imprisonment. So Mother decided to make use of her Polish birth. The problem was she had no documents to prove it.

One morning, when we had news that there was a police raid on the streets and everyone stayed home, I looked into the closet of our apartment hoping to find some family pictures. I was so happy and relieved to find two pictures of Father and next to them a Polish certificate. It must have belonged to a Polish person who lived during the Nazi years in our home. I erased the name and wrote in mother's name. I knew it was illegal but we had nothing to lose.

•   •   •

It was during that time, in the summer of 1945, as we were awaiting the decision from the Polish consul whether that birth certificate would be accepted and we could leave for Poland, that I happened to meet Herr Schwartz.

As I was walking on the Ring-Platz, listening to the news from the front line about the advances of the Soviet army against the Nazis coming from the speakers of the Magistrate building, my eyes suddenly caught a glimpse at a man from a distance walking towards me. His face looked very familiar. After a second glance, I could not believe my eyes. "Could it be Herr Schwartz?" I asked myself. As he came closer, my heart started beating faster. It was Herr Schwartz; the man who wanted to hide us during the Nazi period walked right in front of me. He glanced at me and was ready to pass me by. I greeted him, but he looked at me with a puzzled look in his eyes. It was obvious that he had no idea who I was.

"Herr Schwartz," I yelled with an excited voice. He turned around in surprise.

"Do I know you, young man? Who are you?"

"Yes, Herr Schwartz, I am Miliu (my childhood nickname), Herr Marder's son."

Herr Schwartz was dumbfounded. His eyes expressed shock and disbelief. He could not have possibly been able to recognize me. I was certainly not dressed as he used to remember me.

"God! What has happened to you, my son? Where is your father? Is he all right?"

"Father did not survive." We both stood in silence for a while. It seemed that after the shock of seeing me poorly clothed, the greater shock of Father's death was a blow he found difficult to confront. He needed some time to recover. His eyes fixed, stared into emptiness. Finally, he looked at me and tried to hold back his tears.

"Are your mother and sister alive?" I told him they were.

"I want to go home with you; I need to talk to your mother."

I sensed that Herr Schwartz wanted to ask me questions about Transnistria but could not bring himself to do it. At the same time, a sudden need to lean on someone's shoulder and just cry... and cry... came over me. The sight of Herr Schwartz brought out feelings in me, memories of him pleading with Father not to join the deadly exodus... Images of Father and Herr Schwartz in the store... Flashbacks of better times... It was a cold afternoon. I had just returned from school. Dad was concerned that I had not eaten properly that morning since I had been late for school, so he treated me to a slice of bread and butter. I refused to eat it because I didn't like the taste of that particular bread. Father pleaded with me to eat. He made various designs on the butter to enhance the slice's appearance, but I stubbornly refused to eat. Herr Schwartz sat with his usual kind eyes and watched my stubborn behavior. How I wished to have been able to go back in time! How could I have refused that slice of bread? How spoiled I was! But the past was gone and all that was left was the pain of remembering those moments. That scene with Father and the incident with that slice of bread followed me throughout our starving years in Transnistria.

"I guess you want to know what happened to us after you left our house," I turned to Herr Schwartz, trying to reassure him that it was OK for me to speak, and that he would not be imposing by asking me questions. He looked surprised that I was ready to talk to him. We sat down on a bench in the Ring-Platz on the way home. I had no fear of the Soviet police since they did not bother minors. Herr Schwartz was also safe since he had documents. I felt a need to speak to him and unload some of the tensions that weighed heavily on me:

"A few minutes after you left, we were marched to the station and crowded into cattle cars. The rumor that we would be taken to work on farms did not seem real anymore, because if they wanted us to work, we would need to survive that trip. But based on the way they packed us into these cars, it did not look like they cared if we arrived alive. The first thing we had to do before climbing up to those cars was to deliver all personal gold to a spot on the train station. We were warned that anyone found possessing gold would be shot. People began throwing away gold rings, chains and other personal belongings of gold. The train made stops whenever soldiers or trainmen ended their shift. From the signs we were passing we knew that we were heading in the direction of Bessarabia.

"People began dying on the train and they were taken off when the train stopped. The train stopped in Marculesti.[2] I don't remember how long it took us to get there. We were ordered into empty village huts. We discovered that Jews lived there; they were shot and buried, each family in front or back of their houses. Notwithstanding that tragic news, we were relieved to be under a roof again and people began thinking that the Nazis might leave us there and have us work in the fields.

"But after a few days, soldiers on horses arrived and ordered everyone out of the houses. We were marched through muddy fields and no one knew where they would be taking us. As they kept walking us through the fields, a mixture of rain and snow came down and drenched us to the bones. The ground became increasingly muddy and it was extremely difficult to walk. Many people were getting stuck in the mud and could not continue. The soldiers on the horses kept shooting many people who slowed down their walk, so everyone tried to run ahead and avoid the bullets. I remember crying and telling Father that I cannot walk any more, but Father, trying to distract us, holding back his tears, told my sister and me to count the telegraph poles in the field and see how many we were passing. For a while it helped a little, but the walking didn't get easier. On the way, we began passing by bodies on the ground. I saw a leg sticking out of the mud. It had a pink color. I could not tell from the distance whether it was attached to a body since it was partially buried in the mud.

"It finally got dark and we were told to stop in the Casautz forest, where we were going to spend the night. I never thought that resting in a forest in a freezing rainy and windy night would be a relief. We spread out a blanket we still had with us and tried to lie down, but we were so soaked that the blanket did not help. The only memories that stand out in my mind from that night were the sounds of chattering teeth, the stammering sounds of shivering people around

2 A city in northern Moldova.

us and the dull sounds of rifle shots in the dark of the night."

Herr Schwartz looked distraught.

"I remember the last time I saw Father, he was recovering from pneumonia and still had some temperature on the day of your deportation," he said. "How could he have gone through all this in the condition he was in? How awful it must have been for all of you."

"I don't know how he made it to the last destination," I said. "I know that he and mother were hungry and cold because they gave us the blankets and whatever food was left in our sacks. I remember Father saying to a neighbor: 'I don't want to live to see the day my children starve.'

"We left the forest in the morning. I can't remember the number of days it took us to reach a bridge that crossed into Yampol.[3] Some people were assigned to stay there. We considered them 'lucky' because we were exhausted and felt that we could not make it much further. One welcome surprise was the sight of Italian soldiers handing out hot tea to the children.

"It took several days before we reached a little town named Obodovka. There, I remember a huge barn in which we spent the night. Many people had reached the end of their ropes. The next morning we had shocking news that a great Hassidic rabbi and his wife had decided to end their lives. It was seven kilometers before our final destination. I asked Father how a rabbi, a leader of people, could do something that is forbidden by Jewish law. I remember Father saying to me that 'someday we will talk about it.' That day never came. Father passed away a few weeks later.

"The next day we were marched to Verchovka,[4] a tiny little square of mostly abandoned houses. It was there where we lost Father and where three-quarters of the people who were in our convoy perished."

Herr Schwartz, who sat quietly just listening, asked me hesitatingly how we managed to survive. "What were the conditions there?"

"When we arrived, about 50 people settled in a room we found. It was a small room with two windows that the people boarded up, hoping it would protect us from freezing to death. We were able to secure some straw from outside and used it as beds. There was no

---

3 *Where we crossed the Dniester river into Transnistria.*
4 *This camp in the Ukraine was our final destination.*

room to move, only to lie down."

"What did you do about food, were you given any?" Herr Schwartz wanted to know.

"No food was given. As soon as we arrived, an epidemic of typhoid broke out and people were also dying of cold and hunger. Those who survived the first winter took chances with their lives and sneaked out into the neighboring villages to offer some work for a piece of bread, or pick up an ear of corn or potato that was left in the fields. But it took a winter for us to recover enough strength and be able to stand up and walk. Mother was the only one in our family who did not get sick. She told us later that she had typhoid as a child and for that reason had a stronger immunity to it."

I sensed that Herr Schwartz wanted to know about Father, but didn't dare ask me.

"Father tried to hold on to his strength, but after a few weeks he became very weak and developed a very high fever. There was a doctor in our group, but he had no medicine. Father was lying semiconscious for several days until one morning we realized we had lost him. He lay there with glazed eyes. I was convinced that God wouldn't let him die and kept waiting for him to wake up..."

Herr Schwartz seemed lost for words. His face was pale and expressed agony and distress. He then turned to me. I saw tears in his eyes. He projected compassion and a warmth I had not experienced in a long time. During those years, there was no time for expressions of sympathy and compassion. All our energies were directed at survival.

"Father will be with you always," he said, embracing me. I felt his warmth and wanted to open my feelings up to him.

"Yes," I responded, "Father proved it to me. He came back to me, and thanks to him I am still alive."

"What do you mean, my child?"

"It happened right after he died. I was lying next to him watching him, hoping for any sign of life. I was ill with high fever and fell into a deep sleep. Father appeared to me in a dream. He was dressed in his holiday clothing and looked so happy. He smiled at me. I became ecstatic and yelled out, 'Father is alive, Father is alive!' I wanted to tell him how much I loved him and how happy I was to see him, but he motioned with his hand that there was no need to say anything. Instead, he stretched out his hand towards my mouth and with a big, reassuring smile he said: 'Here, eat this little piece of Matzah.[5] Don't worry. All will be well.'

"Do you know what Matzah is?" I asked Herr Schwartz.

"Yes, my son, I do."

"Well, I tasted the piece of Matzah and woke up."

Herr Schwartz seemed touched. "This is an incredible story. You loved your father so much that you were able to reach out to him in another world. Please tell me what happened after."

"When I woke up and saw Father lying dead next to me—so many people were dying that it took some time for the dead to be buried—I realized that the few moments of happiness were only a dream."

I reached a point where I could no longer continue and Herr Schwartz noticed it. We got up from the bench and resumed our walk home.

Herr Schwartz had a clear picture of our situation. Having been aware that the Transnistria survivors returned to completely plundered, empty homes (if they were lucky enough to find them unoccupied), he needed no further information. He was ready to help us, but those were economically difficult times even for people who had not been in the camps.

I brought Herr Schwartz home. At the sight of Herr Schwartz, Mother began crying. It was an outburst of sobbing locked up inside her throughout those years, when crying was a luxury she could not afford. I could not bear the sound of her crying and had to run out of the house.

Leaving Our Hometown

After meeting Herr Schwartz, Mother received permission for us to go to Poland. From there we were hoping to eventually be able to join Mother's family in the United States. Unfortunately, once we left Czernowitz, we lost all contact with this kind and wonderful man.

I wonder whether Herr Schwartz ever had a chance to leave the Soviet Union and live out his years in a normal environment, free

---

5 Unleavened bread eaten on Passover.

of fear and insecurity. I was about 14 years old when I saw him for the last time. Those moments of our surprise encounter will stay with me for as long as I live, as will the memories of Father's unshakable belief in the goodness of mankind, which he and Herr Schwartz so strongly shared.

Although I had not lost faith in the existence of God, my complete trust in His system of justice and kindness had suffered crushing blows. A sense of deep disappointment had permeated my whole being throughout our years in Transnistria. When Father died, the child in me felt hurt more by God than by people. I had already found out not to expect much from the world. During those years, I had accumulated in my young mind questions about God too—questions that no one could answer for me: If God is kind, how could He have permitted these tragedies to happen? How could He have permitted Father's untimely, tragic death and the destruction of so many other lives?

Leaving for Poland

As the train going to Poland started rolling out of the station, people were relieved to say goodbye to the Soviet Union, yet not without mixed feelings. Everyone was certain that this was their final exit without a chance to ever return to their favored city again. No one who was ever able to leave the Soviet Union during the Stalin era would have dreamed of being able to return. But there seemed to have been a need to reminisce about the good days their beloved hometown had offered them. Czernowitz had been their home, their place of birth, the city where they were married, where their children were born and went to school, and where they had planned to live for the rest of their lives. At the same time they had experienced so much suffering both in the past, during the Nazi period, and so much fear and injustice during the Soviet regime, that to stay would have constituted living in a continued state of uncertainty and fear.

I was preoccupied with my own thoughts and could not help thinking about Father's burial place somewhere in the woods outside Verchovka (which I knew I would never be able to find, even if I had access to the area) and his devoted friend Herr Schwartz, whom I would most probably never see again to show him our deepest gratitude.

I thought of the mention in the scriptures that man was created in God's image. That concept made me feel safe until I came in contact with another world—a world I had not been aware of. During our inhuman experiences, I had great difficulty understanding that concept in the light of the realities we were facing. So many people who looked human did what no wild animal ever would do. Only less than a handful of individuals came to my mind that fit the description of being in God's image.

Sitting in the train as we were leaving Czernowitz, the world of my father and my childhood, I could not help contemplating Herr Schwartz's heroic readiness to help during those times of tragedy and danger. I wondered what kind of image Herr Schwartz was credited with up in heaven. What common ground is there between the nobility and goodness of a person like Herr Schwartz and that of regular people?

There was so much I wished to do for him. I dreamed about finding him again after we found a home somewhere, saving him from the Soviet Union, providing comfort for him during his aging years and doing everything possible to make his life pleasant; but, alas, it was only a dream. Any thought about possible contact with Herr Schwartz was futile. I had to face the sad fact that I would never be able to see him again. There was no possibility of ever coming back to the Soviet Union as a visitor... certainly not to Czernowitz, which was off-limits to visitors (even in later years). All that was left for me to do was to pour my heart out and pray for him; so I made up a prayer for him—a prayer of a 14-year-old—and it went more or less as follows:

Dear God, please take good care of Herr Schwartz. He deserves your special attention. He is as rare as a diamond in the sand. Please guard him from those who are credited with being born in your image, but don't deserve that credit. Please remember his goodness, his dignity and courage. I wish him a long, happy life, but when the time will arrive for him to go to heaven, may he find his rest under your divine wings. Maybe you could appoint him as a counsel for your angels; he may have much to teach them about goodness on Earth. I remember learning that your angels occupy themselves singing praises to You in Heaven. Please remember that while they were busy singing, Herr Schwartz was ready to put his life at risk, trying to shield the lives of his Jewish friend and his family.

You created the world and you know that there is no more difficult task than being an angel on Earth. So, please, take very, very good care of this very special human angel who does honor to Your image.

Thank you, God!

From a distance, the locomotive spewed out a distressing, shrieking whistle. After several bumps back and forth, our car was jolted out of its position and began moving. With clinking sounds and wheels grinding, the train gradually maneuvered its way out of the station. With each passing second, the train created new distances between the past of my childhood years and an unknown future.

Inside the car, the talking had ceased and there was sudden silence. Everyone wanted to be left with their own thoughts and feelings as the train began moving out of the city. Through the cracks of the cattle car (yes, the Soviet government sent us out in "style"), a new panorama of lush green fields and lovely countryside unfolded. It made me feel sad knowing how beautiful the area we lived in was, and how nice it could have been to continue our lives in our hometown and its surroundings had it been a more peaceful world. How tragic it is, I felt, that so many human beings cannot exist without hate.

A formation of soft, plush clouds hovered over the summer horizon, gently converging on each other peacefully. They were sailing along with celestial dignity, and as they were following the direction of our train, I thought of the Bible story about the cloud that followed the ancient Israelites on their exodus from Egypt. I watched them as they glided gracefully through the summery blue sky and my thoughts were with Father and Herr Schwartz.

Looking into those distant clouds, I could fathom the echoes of Father's and Herr Schwartz's voices as they were discussing with their natural, undaunted optimism the future of a better, kinder world.

Father and Herr Schwartz were for me the embodiment of goodness and nobility: Herr Schwartz, because of his goodness, wanted to save our family; and Father, for a twofold noble reason, refused help... first, because he did not want to endanger his friend, and second, because he did not wish to be an exception to the fate that befell his community and people.

After we left Czernowitz, we never saw Herr Schwartz nor heard from him again. Herr Schwartz was in my eyes more than a righteous man. Many people live righteous lives for themselves and their families. But few are ready to put their lives on the line to save the lives of a friend and his family. Herr Schwartz redeemed my faith in mankind. No one could ask more, even from a heavenly angel.

*The apartment building in Czernowitz where the author and his
family lived until they were taken to Transnistria.*

The Skulener Rebbe
Profile of a Saintly Man

The rabbi sat in his study room deep in thought. In front of him on the table were several holy books. His son opened the door carefully and brought him a glass of water. We, the children, were waiting at the door to come in for a shiur—a class.

"Please have a glass of water, Father. You must have some! You ate very little and the doctor said you must eat more and have more liquids."

The Rabbi lifted his head as if he woke up from a dream, took the glass from his son, made a blessing over the water and took a sip.

"Please, Father, take another sip."

But the Rabbi was preoccupied. "God," he said in a quiet, prayerful tone of voice, "the number of children we took reached over a hundred. My faith in You is strong. You will not abandon them. You are called the God of widows and orphans. They went through hell on Earth. Some of them saw their mothers and fathers beaten and killed in front of their eyes. Others were saved from that torture by being separated from their parents before they were killed. I just witnessed Menahem, one of the youngest children we just picked up from a kind Christian family who gave him shelter embracing the tree in the yard, crying. It broke my heart when I heard him ask the tree, 'Please tell me; where is my mother? Where is my father? Please tell me where they are!'"

"God," the Rabbi prayed, "Please give me the strength to provide for these children and be a good father to them. They have no one else left in this world but You. I am not as strong as I used to be. Please, God of orphans, help me to take care of them!"

The Rabbi stopped and realized that we were waiting for him and motioned for us to come in. We knew he was worried about the children and what was going to happen to them after his upcoming arrest. His so-called "transgression" consisted of caring for the orphans and giving them a home. The Soviet regime wanted to have complete control over children, so they considered the Rabbi's activities treason against the state. Someone in the government who respected his humanity advised him that he better make use of a rare opportunity to leave the Soviet Union. The Soviet government permitted Polish-born people to return to their country of origin and papers had been made out for the Rabbi to be on the only civilian train designated to leave the Soviet Union so he could avoid arrest. His wife and his friends tried to convince him to make use of that rare chance.

I began spending most of the time in Rabbi Portugal's home soon after our family, along with other survivors from Transnistria, returned to our hometown. Upon our return, I felt lost and demoralized and walked the streets aimlessly until I eventually came in contact with Rabbi Portugal. A friend of my father who must have observed my emotional struggle to keep afloat after Father's death arranged for me to see Rabbi Portugal.

Rabbi Zyssie Portugal, also referred to as The Skulener,[1] took care of orphans whose parents were killed by the Nazis. He and his wife housed them, fed them and treated them like their own children. They often slept on the floor in order to accommodate a new arrival.

When I came to see him, I was 14 years old. "I am so happy to see you," he greeted me with his shining kind eyes. "I remember you when you were little and Father brought you with your little violin and you played for me. Do you remember?" He stopped for a moment. "Are you continuing with the violin?" I told him I was not.

---

1 *Skulen refers to the Hasidic dynasty founded by Rav Eliezer Zusia Portugal, who was born in Sculeni, a town in pre-war Romania.*

He looked at me with his kind, loving eyes without saying a word. That loving look made me ask Mother if she could possibly somehow get me a violin. Although I was not in a frame of mind to restart studying music, at least I had a violin. It served at that time more as a reminder of better years than as a means of recovering the years I had lost.

The conditions under which Rabbi Portugal helped an extraordinary amount of orphans may seem unreal in normal times. Strangely, one of the factors "enabling" Rabbi Portugal to help the children (although under threat of arrest and deportation to Siberia or the Donbas coal mines) was the chaotic situation in Czernowitz immediately after the Nazis retreated. The Soviet army was still fighting on the front lines with Germany. The newly appointed Soviet local government still lacked the infrastructure to establish a record of its residents and their addresses. From the many thousands who were sent to Transnistria, only a minority survived. Those who did manage to return to their old homes were in danger of being arrested since they had no documents permitting them to enter their hometown. Soviet police closely guarded the streets. They made frequent raids and arrested anyone without documents. Since the survivors of the camps had no documents, they were the most vulnerable to be arrested and deported. Children, however, were left alone and able to walk the streets freely.

Rabbi Portugal lived in a housing complex whose apartments faced a courtyard. Most of those apartments had once belonged to Jewish people who perished in Transnistria. The Rabbi put the children in the abandoned apartments. The proximity of the apartments to each other helped him, with the assistance of his wife, his son and a few friends, to oversee the children, feed them and care for them. His help went for a time unnoticed. When the police began finding out about it, he was in danger of being arrested at any moment.

Fortunately, for as long as it lasted, someone among the Russians in the police department sympathized with the Rabbi's kindness and turned a blind eye on his work. However, a time came when they were no longer able to do so.

When Rabbi Portugal found these children—or they found him—they had no parents, but sometimes relatives would show up and claim them. Those relatives—and their numbers grew as Rabbi Portugal's work became known throughout the area and its surroundings—were grateful to the Rabbi and joined hands to help him as much as they could toward the care of his children.

Aside from his admirers and the community of survivors who tried to help him, two devotees stood out in my memory. They moved into that apartment complex and became a part of his family. One was Rebbe Zalmen Horowitz, also known as the Potoker Rav. He had a son named Shmuel, who was my age and presently lives in Brooklyn. Rabbi Horowitz and his son miraculously survived by running away from their hiding place as Nazi soldiers pursued them. When the solders shot at them from a distance, they fell to the ground—the father on top of the child. They did not move and the soldiers considered them dead. I do not know how he and his son made it to Czernowitz after the liberation of this area. He moved in to the apartment complex where Rabbi Portugal lived and helped him care for the children. Another person who stands out in my mind was Salpeter, a middle-aged man, who was either a convert or Baal T'shuva.[2] All we knew about him was what he had told us: that he had been an atheist in his younger years and then became observant. His devotion to the children was remarkable. His tall stature was imposing, and his kind nature encouraged the children to seek his help in solving their childish disputes.

When I think of Rabbi Portugal, the closest description that comes to my mind is the word Saint. His physical appearance lacked all the attributes which society normally associates with strength and authority. He was a spiritual giant with a big soul dwelling in a small, frail body. His soft-spoken voice could only be heard with effort and his lifestyle was simpler than one might imagine. His face had a pallid complexion, but it radiated an uncommon flow of warmth and love for people. I can still see him standing in his uniquely meek posture, surrounded by children. He always walked with his head inclined, as if he carried the weight of the world's problems on his shoulders. To say that he was humble would be a

---

2 *A person who becomes religiously observant.*

major understatement. The subject of his modesty was once mentioned in his presence, and I remember him saying with a giggle: "To be modest implies having something to be modest about. I have no such worries."

When people came to seek his advice, he received them in an informal manner to make them feel comfortable. Having been one of a group of children who lived with their families but frequented his home, I would sometimes be sent into his study to serve tea to a visiting guest who came to discuss a problem. He listened to his visitor while keeping his eyes on a holy book, and only from time to time would he glance at the person to assure him or her of his attentiveness. It was obvious even to me as a teenager that he avoided revealing his deep insight into people's problems, thus enabling them to open up and be less self-conscious.

He made sure that the orphans living with him would feel completely at home. He addressed each one as "my child," and they felt it natural to call him "Tate" ("Father" in Yiddish). Their needs were always given preference over any other work, including his beloved activity of studying the holy books. No matter how engrossed he was in his studies, he was always ready for the children. Whenever a child needed his attention, he would pick him up, put him on his lap and talk to him in his special affectionate way. There were also teenage children—some with deep emotional scars—who would have been considered unmanageable by others. To Rabbi Portugal, there were no problem children. His approach to them was one of unconditional love and respect. His affectionate manner was disarming. Love and care were the medicines he believed would eventually cure all their emotional scars, and it did. Even some of their physical ailments somehow dissipated in time.

Caring personally for the emotional and physical needs of that large number of children, especially under the watchful eyes of Soviet authorities, would have posed overwhelming problems for most people, but Rabbi Portugal never showed signs of impatience with the children nor fear for himself. His face, indeed his whole being, radiated kindness, love and peace.

The Soviet Officer and his Son

One of several incidents I witnessed serves as an example of the powerful impact that his personality had even on strangers meeting him for the first time. Rabbi Portugal was on his way home after visiting a sick person. (Luckily, he had identification papers so he was able to walk without being arrested on the street.) He passed by one of the main plazas in the center of town known as the Ring Platz. A Soviet officer, who was sitting on a bench with his son, suddenly stood up at the sight of the Rabbi and greeted him with a bow, as one would react having seen a great dignitary. The child seemed surprised.

"Father, why are you standing up," the boy asked his father, pointing to Rabbi Portugal.

"I don't know who this man is, but he certainly is no ordinary person."

We were three boys accompanying Rabbi Portugal on that walk. None of us were surprised at the incident because we were used to seeing people react in similar ways at the sight of this humble and kind man.

Those of us who returned with one parent were just as welcome as orphans were in his house. We studied there, and, to him, we were also "his" children. Studying with Rabbi Portugal did by no means suggest coming to a shiur[3] and leaving afterward. His was an open house. The children living on the outside became aware that it was normal to stay in Rabbi Portugal's home as long as they wished, and every child wanted to do just that. To be there and feel the Rabbi's love and concern, his compassion and warmth, was just the right medicine for all of us youngsters there. We all felt a need to recover from the emotional numbness we had acquired in Transnistria in order to survive. Following those gruesome years of internment, we were all drawn by his goodness and love.

It was during those visits that I became aware of the Rabbi's serious economical hardships and the gigantic task he and his wife faced daily in trying to provide food for his big household and visiting strangers. When his great compassion became known in the city of Czernowitz and its vicinity, people in need came not only to seek his advice but also just to eat a meal. His wife, no less devoted

3 *Torah lesson.*

to his work, faced not only the difficult challenge of providing enough food for the large family and visitors, but also keeping up with the Rabbi's limitless generosity.

Mrs. Portugal, or the Rebbetzin, as we knew her, was a middle-aged, rather peppy lady of small build, with a radiant twinkle in her almond eyes. Her authoritative voice compensated handsomely for her small body, which always moved with an energetic, jovial bounce.

To save some extra money for Sabbath meals, the Rebbetzin used to keep spare change in a kitchen drawer. But the Rabbi would always use some of it for people in need who came to see him during the course of the week. Every Thursday, before going to the market to shop for the Sabbath, Mrs. Portugal would take out the saved coins from the drawer to help supplement her perennial shortage of money for shopping.

One day a curious thing happened. We were in the midst of a Talmud class, learning from the section of Baba Metziah in the tractate Berachot about laws relating to claims on found items. Rabbi Portugal began reading a section dealing with fruits or coins, etc., found in public domain, and under what circumstances such finds would belong to the finder. He suddenly stopped and smilingly commented:

"I consider the house we live in as public domain." We were puzzled by both his statement and by the smile on his face when he made it. But, not long after, the mystery unfolded itself. Rebbetzin Portugal burst into the Rabbi's "study," (a room containing a plain old table and chairs) complaining that the money in the drawer was gone.

"I know who the thief is," she confronted her husband, with loving agitation in her voice.

"What am I going to do with you?" she complained. "You are a man with loose fingers!"

The class broke into laughter, because it was no secret to us that whenever someone in need came to see him, he would go to the kitchen drawer, take out the needed money, and give it to them. The Rabbi, with his usual calm and kind smile on his face, tried to pacify his wife: "Yes, my wife, it was I who took the money. A widow came in yesterday and needed some money to feed her sick boy. If you would have seen the pain on her face, you would have done the same. Don't worry! I am confident that God will provide us with our needs for the Sabbath."

The Rebbetzin walked out, speechless, knowing there was no point arguing with her husband. Although we reacted with laughter to the Rebbetzin's complaint, we were nevertheless concerned that there might be a shortage of food for them on the Sabbath. After all, Saturday was around the corner. How would they be able to make up for the missing money?

After the class was over, the Rabbi, as was his custom, retreated to a corner and continued his own studies, unconcerned, as always, about money matters. We later understood the reason why the Rabbi categorized their apartment, including the contents in the kitchen drawer, as public domain. He regarded everything in his home as public property because he felt that everything in his possession must be shared with others. Rabbi Portugal would always remind us:

God is the only owner in the Universe, as it is written, Ki li kol Haaretz—The whole world is mine. All of us living creatures are guests in this world, and we all live on borrowed time. Everything we use for our sustenance is given to us on loan by the Creator, including our very lives.

A few hours after the kitchen money incident, the Rabbi was about to begin his afternoon prayers. The doorbell rang. A guest had just arrived from out of town and was hoping to be able to stay over in the Rabbi's house for the Sabbath. (It was very common for guests to stay in Rabbi Portugal's home. Somehow, room was always made for them.) Upon hearing the story about the "missing" money, the guest more than replenished it. At a time when both food and money were so scarce in the city, this happening was nothing short of a miracle.

We learned of Rabbi Portugal's urgent need to leave Soviet Russia when one summer afternoon in 1945, an officer from the Soviet secret police showed up at the door.

"Is Gospodin[4] Portugal home?" he asked with urgency in his voice, "I need to talk to him; it is very important." One of the children who opened the door led him to the Rabbi. While

---

4 *Mister in Russian.*

pretending not to understand, the boy parked himself at an audible distance, looking into a book. It soon became known to us that the officer warned the Rabbi that there was an order out for his arrest. The Rabbi was calm, but soon we began feeling an atmosphere of nervousness in the house. The Rebbetzin started packing, and it became obvious that she was packing things for her husband only. We also noticed that the Rabbi's son was putting holy books in sacks. Beyond that, things were going on as usual. The Rabbi attended to his children as he always did and the house continued its daily routine.

Since the warning of the Rabbi's arrest coincided with an agreement by the Soviet Union to let Polish natives return to their country, the only opportunity the Rabbi had to avoid arrest was to leave Soviet Russia on the only civilian train for Poland. Rabbi Portugal had two days to decide whether to leave his children or take the chance to be arrested.

Most Polish citizens who lived in Czernowitz and the surrounding areas already had obtained their permits for leaving. Friends worked hard to get permission for the Rabbi to leave on that train, and finally succeeded. The Rabbi's family and friends were anxious for him to go and be saved from prison; but he did not seem willing to leave. On several occasions he said: "I cannot leave without my children."

Our family—mother, sister and I—were lucky to have obtained permission to leave Soviet Russia since Mother was born in Poland. At the appointed day given us by the authorities, we met at the train station with a few friends and Rabbi Horowitz, who was also leaving for Poland, and boarded the same car. We also secured a place for Rabbi Portugal. One of his older adopted sons brought the Rabbi's "belongings"—a few sacks of holy books—and left them in the car.

The train station was in a state of mass confusion. People rushed and pushed in all directions, trying to climb the cattle cars as quickly as they could because no one knew the exact time the train would be leaving. We waited for the Rabbi. Several people went to look for him throughout the station but he was nowhere to be found. The people in the car became fearful.

"If the train starts moving and Rabbi Portugal is not on it, he will surely be arrested," a woman in the car said with fear in her voice. They knew how urgent it was for him to be on that train.

When Rabbi Portugal did not show up in time, everyone was worried. We knew that the order for his arrest issued by the NKVD[5] was imminent.

"Where is the Rabbi?" another lady asked with anxiety. Rabbi Horowitz tried to calm her.

"Don't worry," he replied, "the Rabbi will be back in time. One must have faith in God. He probably just went to pray at the nearest synagogue. You know," he added reassuringly, "it is written that messengers of good deeds are not harmed."

A young mother burst out with bitterness in her voice: "Too many people in the last few years lost their lives serving God. I just hope that Rabbi Portugal will be safe. A few days after the Nazis entered Czernowitz, my father, Elisha, you remember him?" she asked with a hopeful look on her face waiting for us to tell her that we remembered him. She looked at me. "He used to go to the same synagogue your father went to, remember?"

"Yes," I said. "Of course, I remember him. He had a beautiful voice."

"Do you know," she went on with a painful expression on her face, "that he was on his way to do a good deed. He was shot on his way to the prayer house!"

Rabbi Horowitz tried to change the sad mood.

"Why don't we sit down and study a page of Talmud?" he turned to his son and me, the only young boys in the car. "After all, there is no substitute for learning, especially in a place like this. It would not be very productive to just sit and watch the walls of this cattle car. Look how much light we are getting from the sun. We must make good use of that beautiful light! Isn't it an ideal situation for learning?" he quipped with a jolly smile on his face, trying to lift the spirit of the people in the car.

Rabbi Horowitz was well aware that we were not in a frame of mind to study and his suggestion felt out of place amidst the pandemonium and the worry about Rabbi Portugal that surrounded us.

5 Soviet secret police.

"Come on, let's not be lazy," he chided us good-naturedly. "Since the Rabbi is not here, why don't we do a little studying on our own?"

Reluctantly, we took out a Talmud from one of the sacks, sat down on our luggage and began learning. We were unable to concentrate. Our minds were really on the Rabbi and what was going to happen to him.

As we sat in the car waiting for the Rabbi, the tension increased with each moment of his absence. Since there was no set time given for the train's departure, our waiting was so much more tense. We all loved the Rabbi and restlessly hoped he would show up.

Unfortunately, our hope turned into sad reality. That moment arrived. The locomotive shrieked out several loud whistles and the train began moving out of the station; to our great sorrow, without Rabbi Portugal.

If the Soviet government was not efficient in providing its citizens with their utmost necessities, it certainly excelled in its infamous "reliability" and "discipline" when it came to incarcerating people. In fact, the city of Czernowitz was one of the areas in which the Soviet system was very prompt in carrying out their arrests and deportations. We knew it, and that was why we were so concerned about the Rabbi.

It took one day of travel, and when the train made its first stop for the night in Lublin, Poland, I began to have mixed feelings about the Rabbi's absence in the car. Our car was pelted with stones accompanied by anti-Semitic slurs. Knowing Rabbi Portugal, I was imagining how much pain this saintly, peaceful man would have felt, seeing that only months after the war and the Holocaust, people would still be so poisoned with hate and try to hurt people who, they knew, survived the most inhuman experiences. I had the feeling the Rabbi would have preferred being in prison rather than witness that sight.

When we arrived in Lodz, we and others immediately realized that staying in Poland was out of question for us. The pogrom in Kielce took place at that time. We saw that our lives were in danger and realized that we must leave the country quickly. We knew that we had to cross the borders of Poland and Czechoslovakia to be able to make it to the West, and that there were dangers lurking during such crossings. But at that point we had nothing to lose. There were some tense moments when we crossed the borders. We were able to talk ourselves out of being arrested by crossing the Polish border as Greek refugees, and finally were lucky enough to make it to the U.S. Zone of Germany.

During that time, we had no news about Rabbi Portugal. It was several months after we arrived in Germany while we were in the Displaced Persons Camp Föhrenwald, that we heard the sad news about the arrests of Rabbi Portugal and his son. One of "his" children fled from Soviet Russia and made it to Germany. He told us that the same day we left for Poland, the Rabbi and his son, Yisroel, were arrested and no one knew their whereabouts.

We could not believe that even those heartless Soviet authorities would keep this peaceful man arrested for too long, and hoped he and his son would be released within a short time. We had no news about his wife, who stayed in Czernowitz, and how she managed with the children after the arrest of her husband and son.

As time went by, the silence surrounding his whereabouts gradually erased any hope of his being freed. Those who were informed about the Soviet prison system and its conditions knew that survival within their walls presented an enormous challenge even to the physically sturdy. The chances for Rabbi Portugal's survival, therefore, required nothing short of a miracle.

Years after our family's arrival in the United States, I received news about the Rabbi's release from prison. Apparently, his and his son's whereabouts were eventually discovered. A great number of his "children" and friends managed to flee Soviet Russia and settled in the United States and other Western countries. The stories about his special kindness and heroic deeds to save others became known. Those he helped never forgot their loving father, guide and mentor. After an untiring campaign and great efforts to free the Rabbi, as well as intervention on his behalf from Secretary General of the United Nations Dag Hammarskjold, Rabbi Portugal was finally freed. He was permitted to go to London, and eventually his "children" brought him to New York, where he remained.

He continued his benevolent efforts to the end of his life. There are countless stories that depict his inner goodness. I remember one in particular pertaining to his ongoing work to help people leave Russia. Among the many whom he had rescued was a woman who had previously reported him to the Soviet Authorities for helping his children. Here is what he said when asked why he went through such great efforts to save her:

"You have no idea how much she suffered beforehand, and how tempting the authorities made it for people to be an informer."

A Visit with the Rabbi

A short time after his arrival to the United States, I visited him in his modest apartment in Crown Heights. It became immediately apparent to me that his years in prison had a profound effect on his physical health. I introduced myself.

"Oh, yes," his face lightened up with a warm smile. "Sholem Aleikhem! Thank God for being able to see old friends. How are you?"

I was surprised that he remembered me after all those years.

"I remember when your father paid me visits and brought you along. You were about six years old then; how time flies! I knew your father before you were born. I admired his devotion to helping people."

He had heard that Father refused to be saved by his German friend who had offered to take us to a secret hideout. The Rabbi did not comment on the wisdom or folly of Father's decision. He only said to me, "Your father was a very unusual man."

He wanted to know how I was doing.

"I remember when you started violin lessons. Tell me about yourself." As we sat and talked, it was satisfying for me to see that his spirit was unbroken and his personality pure and untouched. But, unfortunately, his physical condition was not up to maintaining lengthy conversations. I noticed that he was very weak, so I decided it was time to leave, but the rabbi motioned me to stay.

He continued his custom throughout the years to weave into his meetings with visitors a "Dvar Torah"—a thought emanating from the holy scriptures. He began quoting Psalm #23, "God is my shepherd, I shall not want..." etc. When he arrived at the phrase "only goodness and kindness shall follow me all the days of my life," he paused. Closing his eyes, seemingly collecting his thoughts, he continued:

"That sentence poses a question: Why do we pray for goodness and kindness to follow us? Logic dictates that we would happily follow blessings without hesitation. The implication here points to a human predicament. Even though we have been granted the ability to make choices, as we are told, 'I have set before thee life and death; blessings and cursing: therefore choose life,'[6] the right decisions are not always easily discernible to us. Sforno[7] comments on this matter, noting that since Adam and Eve ate the apple from the tree of knowledge, mankind's judgment had become affected. History's tragic pages are a sad proof that human judgment is far from flawless. Our vision is sometimes blurred by looking at matters superficially, tending to hamper us from making choices that are for our own good. There are times when we turn our backs on situations that on the surface may appear unfavorable to us, yet may contain seeds of blessings waiting to be acted upon and ready to bloom and grow. Therefore, we beseech the Almighty to permit situations embodying goodness and blessings we cannot perceive, to follow us, even if out of ignorance we may turn and run away from them."

The Rabbi's effort became more pronounced as he continued talking. Trying to avoid showing the sadness I felt over his condition, I stood up and excused myself. We bid each other goodbye.

"Don't be a stranger; come more often," he said with the same softness in his voice and kindness radiating from his eyes I had been used to throughout the years I had known him. There was a tone of tentativeness in his voice. It seemed as if he felt that his physical presence would not be around much longer.

It was the last time I saw him.

Once in a while during our lifetime, if we are fortunate, we may encounter a person who leaves an indelible imprint on our lives. It is not as much through words that they profoundly inspire us, but through the quality of their lives.

There are many scholars and religious leaders but few—far too few—spiritual giants. Rabbi Portugal was one of those precious few. People referred to him as a "Malakh" (angel or messenger in Hebrew). For those believing that angels are messengers of the

6 (Deut.XXX 19).
7 Hananeel ben Jacob Sforno was a 15th-century scholar of Talmud.

Almighty who perform their missions by divine assignment, there is no doubt that Rabbi Portugal earned a very special place among them; for his missions of love and kindness originated in his own great, beautiful heart and soul. His memory is, and will be, blessed forever by those whose lives he touched.

This true story is dedicated to Howard and Debbie Jonas.

Professor Jan Von Nowak

The professor walked over to the grand piano where his violin was resting, picked it up and handed it to me.

"Here," he said with an annoyed tone: "Here!... Play!..."

I felt embarrassed. How could I, a 17-year-old who had not studied in 10 years, play for this concert violinist? I had not heard a sound of fine music since I was nine when the great George Enescu gave a concert in my hometown. After that, the only "music" I heard was the delirious singing of people in Transnistria before dying.

After my violin was wrenched from my hands by a peasant as we were driven by foot through the muddy fields of Bessarabia, I often wished to, at least, hold a violin, or see one. And here, I finally had one in my hands but felt paralyzed.

I met Professor Nowak in Germany a year after we were freed from Transnistria. Following a long and arduous journey out of the Soviet Union, our family arrived to Föhrenwald, a displaced persons camp in Bavaria, Germany, where we found a safe, temporary haven. It was one of many camps for Holocaust survivors who could not return to their homes. Many, whose loved ones perished in the camps, could not face returning to their places of birth without their families. The wounds of their experiences were too raw. Others refused to return to their birth countries because of the hateful atmosphere they knew they would face.

When, in July 1946, news reached the displaced persons camps that 40 Jewish survivors from the Nazi camps were murdered by local people in a pogrom in the Polish city of Kielce, even those who had considered returning resolved not to go back. They knew that the recent pogrom was not the first and felt it might not be the last.

We felt relieved to finally be settled in Föhrenwald, where we found respite from Soviet persecution and safety from Eastern European post-war anti-Semitism. The camp served also as a place for refugees to recover from the Nazi years and prepare for new lives in countries that would permit them entry.

Meeting Professor Nowak

Meeting Professor Nowak was a complete surprise. It never occurred to me that I would ever meet a musician of that stature. There was no reason to. I had given up the idea of studying the violin long before.

Holding a violin in my hands in the house of the professor, who was known as a violin soloist of high caliber, seemed to me surreal. I could not believe it was happening.

Professor Nowak was a man in his thirties. After seeing his features close up, I recognized his face from the posters announcing his concerts on the billboards in Munich.

He had a small, expressionless face that made one wonder if it could ever turn into a warm smile. He was thin and fidgety. His bulging, brown eyes looked like they were ready to jump out through his thick eyeglass lenses.

Nowak combined a strange mixture of meticulousness with ungainly sloppiness, which was due more to lack of taste than means. He sported a carefully trimmed Hitler-style mustache and several lonely strands of black hair were scrupulously combed towards the back. There his fussiness seemed to have ended. He exhibited a peculiar pleasure in wearing wrinkled sport shirts and shabby pants with shoes to match. And, when he talked, he rarely left out a sentence without a curse.

Curiously, I never remember him showing signs of affinity to music or any other form of art in his daily conversations. He certainly did not match my teenage image of a person with higher level of education.

He spoke German poorly and had a heavy Polish accent. He lived with his wife in the town of Wolfratshausen, about three kilometers from Föhrenwald. It became obvious to me later that he did not seem to have friends in town except for a lady who was a fine pianist and her daughter, who was his student. No one really knew about his general schooling, but his official title was Professor Jan Von Nowak and he was known as far as I could tell for his technically polished performances. Aside from his rigid practicing schedule, I found that he took pleasure sitting in bars and engaging in chatting with the Bavarian peasant folk.

My Friend Mike

Several months after we arrived in Föhrenwald, a school was established and I was able to resume my studies. Although I was not in a frame of mind to study, I went to school knowing how much time I had lost. It was there where Mike and I first met.

Mike and I were considerably different from each other. Mike was sports-oriented and excellent in mathematics. He preferred to conceal his sensitive nature by conducting himself in a who-cares manner. I, on the other hand, was shy and painfully introverted. I still maintained an intense feeling for music, but my dreams about playing the violin had long died. I was interested in literature and poetry, although after the war years I lacked the concentration to read a book from beginning to end.

When Mike found out that I had been "something of a prodigy," as he labeled me, he wondered why, now that the war was over, I did not attempt to resume my music studies. He asked my mother about it, but her answer was that it was up to me. I assume he sensed that it was a touchy subject for me because I never brought up the subject.

Since Camp Föhrenwald was overcrowded, people often took walks to Wolfratshausen, the nearest town to the camp, to see a movie or just enjoy the tree-lined road.

One afternoon, while Mike and I were doing homework, my sister, Eva, returned from Wolfratshausen.

"Guess what," she said, "I just heard very nice violin playing coming from a house in town.

"That person sounds like a very good violinist. I wonder why a violinist of that caliber would live in a small town like that."

"Why not?" I asked, somewhat annoyed.

"You sound irritated," Mike said with a devilish smile on his face. "Maybe you studied too much today. Come on, let's go and see a movie. It's still early enough to go to town."

"What movie are they playing this week?"

"They are playing *The Magic Bow*."

"What is it about?"

"It is about a violinist by the name of Paganini."

"It's OK by me," I said.

Mike had also heard violin playing during one of his walks to town. He knew nothing about music, but liked the sound of the violin. Later, when he found out from my mother that I excelled in violin studies as a child, he decided to take matters in his own hands and try to get me to meet the violinist in Wolfratshausen. When he saw my irritation at the mention of violin, he suspected that I still may have wanted to study violin but something was holding me back. Mike told me later that he overheard me once say: "There are only child prodigies but no teenage ones." He realized that being a teenager, I felt it was too late for me to play the violin again, so he decided to do something about it.

Under the pretense of going to the movies, Mike concocted a plan to get me to meet Professor Nowak. He apparently found out his name and apartment number on one of his visits to town.

A Surprise Walk

It was a beautiful, bright afternoon, perfect for a walk to town. A mild breeze carried the wonderful fragrance from the pine trees along the road and nearby fields, delighting the senses—the kind of day that lifts the spirit. Mike and I were in a jovial mood, so we ran part of the way. As we arrived in town, Mike slowed down his pace one block before the movie house.

"Why are you slowing down," I wanted to know, "we still have a little way to the movie house."

"I need to make a stop here for a minute," he said, poker-faced.

"What for?"

Mike did not answer. He rushed to ring a front doorbell, leaving no time for explanations.

"We need to rush, otherwise we'll be late for the movie," he said.

A thin-looking man with a black mustache and a pair of nervous eyes staring at us through heavy-rimmed lenses appeared at the door.

"What do you want," he asked us with an annoyed tone.

I was puzzled. I thought the man expected Mike.

"My friend wants to talk to you," Mike said to the professor.

"What do you want to talk to me about?" the man asked me with obvious irritation. I was shocked and embarrassed and didn't know what this was all about. His question left me speechless. I felt like running away as fast as my feet could carry me, run to the movie house and disappear in the crowd. Mike noticed it and hurriedly jumped in with an answer.

"My friend once played the violin," he said to the professor. "I think he wants to continue to study." I blushed and did not know whether I felt more embarrassed or frustrated with Mike's aggressive way of bringing me there.

The professor looked us over with suspicion and his eyes expressed anger mixed with annoyance. What do I need this for, I asked myself. Why did Mike throw me into this?

The professor thought for a moment and after some hesitation opened the door and said, grudgingly, "Follow me upstairs."

As we walked up the steps I complained to Mike: "What do you think you are you doing, bringing me up here and not telling me anything about it? How could you do that?" Mike did not answer. He was satisfied that he achieved his goal of bringing me to meet the violinist.

We entered his studio. It was a dark, small-sized room. Upon entering it, one could not help but notice an excessive amount of hunting-trip mementos of stuffed animal heads crowding the walls. The only visible indication of his association with music was the presence of a finely polished violin. It was well wrapped in a dark, silken piece of material inside an open violin case resting over a grand piano. The top of the piano was covered with a colorful, heavy piece of oriental tapestry. An elaborately carved antique wooden music stand stood nearby with a book on it marked *Wieniawsky* Concerto. On one end of the room stood a sofa bed and next to it, a small, antique coffee table with two porcelain ashtrays filled with ashes and several empty packs of cigarettes. An armchair barely fit into the leftover space on the opposite side of the bigger sofa.

The sour-faced professor pointed to the sofa for us to sit down and settled himself on the armchair, reached into his shirt pocket, pulled out a pack of cigarettes and opened it up with the edginess of an addict deprived of his drug for an intolerable period of time. His hands were shaking as he tried to light his cigarette with an anxious, almost painful expression on his face. While looking us over with examining glances, he began asking me questions about my studies.

"At what age did you begin studying the violin?" he asked me with a harsh tone, as if he was accusing me of a crime.

"At the age of six." I was so uncomfortable I could not recognize my own voice.

"And how long did you continue studying?"

"Until the age of ten."

"Why did you stop?" he continued with an unpleasant tone.

"Because the war broke out and the Nazis came in to our town and Jews could no longer study in the conservatory."

"Why didn't you continue to study privately?"

"Because we were taken to a camp in Transnistria."

"Where is that?"

"We were sent to an area in the Ukraine, which the Nazis called Transnistria."

The professor looked even more annoyed than before when we came in.

"Why didn't you study there?"

I was at a loss finding myself having to explain why I did not study violin in a concentration camp. Is he so ignorant or does he play games with me, I wondered.

"There was no music in the concentration camp. We did not know from day to day whether we would be alive. Our main preoccupation was to find food to survive. Most people died of hunger, cold and typhoid."

The professor looked uncomfortable and changed the subject.

"Where do you live now? he asked me.

"We come from Föhrenwald."

"You come from that D.P. camp, eh?"

His voice sounded especially unfriendly when he asked that question. The professor's impoliteness began bothering Mike. Annoyed, Mike defiantly whispered in my ear, "It's not his business!"

I felt that I must show respect to the professor, so I answered his questions quietly:

"Are your parents with you?"

"My mother and my sister survived. We are together now."

Throughout our visit the professor seemed consumed by an incessant indulgence in chain smoking, lighting up one cigarette after another. His wiry, nervous personality did not permit him to sit still. He sat moving his body from one side to another as if the seat's tacks had been stapled with the needles upwards. His favorite subjects, it turned out, were fishing, hunting and movies. But he also mentioned the war, albeit passingly during the conversation.

"Hitler could have won the war if he hadn't tried to swallow up the whole world so fast." The professor said it with a bitter smile that made him look regretful about the Nazis having lost the war.

I watched the professor. His strange attitude to serious matters left even young fellows like us with the impression that his myopic view was not limited to his eye condition only. Although he must have spent many years to become a violinist of stature, he nevertheless gave us the impression of a man with a greater addiction to cigarettes than a devotion to music. He certainly didn't match my image of an artist. He did not talk much about music and certainly did not appear like a person interested in literature or art. In short, he seemed a phenomenon beyond my understanding. I was surprised by the professor's coarse language, which reminded me of Bier Halle drinkers I saw sitting at tables outside Munich bars. I could not reconcile the professor's deportment with the image of a man who carried a "professor" title, and whose name had an upper-society title like "Von" attached to it. Perhaps his crudeness was an affectation, I thought, but underneath his rudeness he must be a very cultured person.

I also could not understand why the professor could hardly speak German. It was heavily laden with sounds of the Polish language. As a matter of fact, at times it was difficult for me to tell whether he spoke German or Polish. Judging by the way he was struggling with his German, the professor must have been living in Germany for a very short time, I thought.

Mike and I also wondered how the professor was able to move to Germany from Poland unless he claimed to be a Volks Deutsche (a person of German origin), since the Nazis, as far as we knew, only allowed such categories of people to move to and live in Germany.

After conversing with us for a while, the professor cut short his talk, walked over impatiently to the violin case resting over the piano, took out the violin and handed it to me. (Little did I realize that the instrument he handed me was a Guarnerius violin, nor was I knowledgeable enough to appreciate the importance of such a rare, high-quality instrument.)

"Play!" He commanded. I stood paralyzed, but the professor was insistent.

"Play! What are you afraid of? No one is going to bite you!"

There was nowhere to run. I felt caught between the immense pleasure of feeling the violin in my hands again and the trepidation of confronting the dreaded moment of truth awaiting me once I tried to play. I started putting my fingers on the strings and looked apologetically at the professor, but his insistence made me realize that there was no way out. I made several attempts to play and stopped in frustration, but the professor showed no sympathy and motioned me to continue. Gradually, flashes from my childhood's musical past began emerging finding expression through the fingers. Although I was enjoying the sound of the violin, I also suffered the traumatic experience of realizing how much I had lost.

Suddenly, memories from my Transnistria years came back. To fight hunger, I used to sing the violin compositions I had learned.

The pieces I used to play began reappearing in my memory. I started playing some Schubert, and as I played, much of what I had previously learned began coming forth, reentering my mind in a procession of fragmentary snippets, like old friends suddenly showing up one by one out of nowhere. The professor sat, on his armchair, legs crossed, watching intently, making no comments. I kept stopping and the professor urged me to go on. It felt like an eternity, but the playing could not have taken more than ten minutes. Finally, I gave up in frustration.

"Well, what's the problem, young fellow?" the professor asked with a tone of dissatisfaction and impatience. I apologized.

"I am sorry, professor, but that's all I can do."

"O.K., O.K..." he said impatiently. He paused for a moment.

"I gather you have a violin."

"No. I don't."

"Why not?"

"I had one, but it was taken away from me on the Polish border."

The professor had a smirk on his face and I could not figure out whether he did not like the fact that the violin was taken away from me, or if he was annoyed that it was done by Polish border guards.

"Would you like to come back?"

"I think so." My voice must have sounded tentative.

"Nobody is forcing you, you know. Come only if you want to... but remember... only if you want to come."

He got up restlessly from his chair.

"On second thought," he corrected himself, "you'd better come with your mother. Do you think your mother could come to see me?"

"Yes, I think she could."

"Well then, tell her I want to talk to her. Tomorrow afternoon will be fine."

"I will tell her."

We got up to leave. "Danke, Herr Professor," Mike and I yelled out in unison. I felt relieved it was over.

"Auf Wiedersehen," the professor answered, this time with a slight smile on his face.

On our way back, I felt like giving Mike an argument for putting me through all this, but the incident was over. On the other hand, I was grateful to him for helping me realize that there was still some desire left in me to study music. I had to admit to myself that just holding the violin was a joy I had not experienced in a long time in spite of the unpleasantness, embarrassment and discomfort of having to confront my terribly rusty playing. I decided to tell Mother about the incident immediately upon my return.

"You know what?" I said, feeling somewhat awkward for bringing up a subject that had not been discussed in years.

"Remember when Eva returned from Wolfratshausen and said she heard violin playing coming from one of the houses?"

"What about it?" Mother wanted to know.

"Well, Mike and I stopped by the man's house. He is a concert violinist. He had me play for him and he wants to see you."

I watched Mother. She was quiet and showed no reaction. I knew she was well aware how much I lost during the war years, both in general and musical education. She knew how difficult violin study is under normal circumstances, and how much harder it would be for me to make up for those lost years. I did not expect a positive answer from her, but to my surprise she was agreeable.

"We'll go tomorrow to see him," she said with a bland expression on her face. The next day, we went to the professor's studio.

Professor Nowak seemed different than on the first day Mike and I met him. He greeted Mother with a cordial bow and asked us to sit down. His demeanor changed to that of a refined man of high society. I was amazed at the professor's changed deportment and suspected that the presence of a lady may have caused him to act in a more refined manner than he did the day before.

The professor immediately addressed himself to Mother:

"I will come straight to the point, Madame," he said in a businesslike fashion. "Yesterday I listened to your son play. He must continue his violin studies immediately. He lost very valuable time and cannot afford to wait longer. The boy has talent. I cannot foretell his progress, but he must have a chance to make use of his musical ability. If it is agreeable to you, I could start him off even before he acquires a violin. It will be free of charge. Unfortunately, I will not be able to teach him for an extended period of time because I will be giving Master classes in Frankfurt and will be there most of the season. But, he must start now! There is no time to lose. Would you agree to his resuming violin lessons?"

"I guess he should continue with his music," Mother said reluctantly. An appointment was made for the first lesson.

It seems that the professor's talk had an effect on the family. Outside the camp, my brother-in-law, Meyer, was able to buy a student violin. Finally I had a violin again.

My lessons with Professor Nowak began and continued for several months until he had to leave for his master classes in Frankfurt. Actually, the classes with the professor were not lessons in the real sense of the word. They amounted more to experimental attempts by the professor to see how much progress I could make within the short period of time he was going to teach me, so he pushed ahead, assigning me works way beyond my level.

"I am going to give you a piece by Paganini to work on. Do you know who Paganini was?"

"No," I confessed uneasily with embarrassment over my utter ignorance of anything related to music. "I just saw a movie about Paganini and know that he was a great violinist."

The professor noticed my embarrassment and ignored it. "He was a great Italian virtuoso, a sensation in his time, who revolutionized violin playing. He had a fantastic violin technique and his compositions are not easy to play. I am giving you one of his pieces and I want to see how you will handle it. It is one of his Caprices."

"What is a Caprice?" I asked shyly.

"A Caprice is a short musical composition. A lot of them are difficult. It will help your fingers gain more flexibility. Now go back to camp and practice it."

Not having heard music, I obviously had no idea how difficult that piece was and accepted the professor's judgment. I began practicing the violin with increasing dedication.

Occasionally I heard the professor play and was amazed at his accomplished playing. I was not knowledgeable enough at that time to judge his level of artistry, but was highly impressed with the professor's technical accomplishments on the violin.

As the lessons progressed, Professor Nowak began communicating with me on matters outside music. Once, after the end of a lesson, as I was closing the violin case, the professor reproached me jokingly for "not being a good Jew":

"I just cannot understand you, Samuel. What kind of a Jew are you? How come you are not interested in money?"

It sounded awfully weird to me, but I disregarded him. Such and similar comments became more frequent as time went on but were always expressed lightheartedly and affectionately. I was not used to "good-natured," lighthearted, smiling anti- Semitism. As I got to know him, I thought of his obsession with "The Jews" as a twisted, perverted, attitude that does no one harm. Mike and I called it jokingly Antisemititis—the sickness without available pills for relief. Since he always made his comments in a kidding, good-natured manner, it did not seem to affect me negatively. I did not feel evil in a smile. I guess other people might have reacted differently, but rightly or wrongly, neither Mike nor I took him seriously. Mike came once in a while to my lessons and also heard the professor's meaningless statements. On the way back we would joke about them and dismiss his talks as meaningless jabber.

Professor Nowak belonged to a not-so-rare lot of prejudiced people with a semi-conscience who, somehow, still find a need to prove to themselves (and others) that their brand of prejudice is intellectually sane. Such people wish to demonstrate their "objectivity" by finding an "exceptional" person from a group they dislike or even by claiming friendship with them. Some anti-Semites do the same.

That offers them justification for their generalizations so they can continue to stick to their favorite theories about those they dislike: that they are "all the same; that they are all up to something." In the case of anti-Semites, one of their favorite theories is that there is a Jewish plan in the works to conspire against the world. Of course, there may be an exception here or there. It looked like the professor may have chosen me for that "role."

One day after a lesson, the Professor asked me to go fishing with him. I hate fishing, but went along with him to keep him company. On the way, we passed by a Catholic Church. I noticed that Professor Nowak was crossing himself as we passed by. I felt like asking him how it is possible to love one Jew (Jesus) and feel the way he feels towards all other Jews, but decided to keep quiet rather than entering into nonsensical talk. We also passed by a bar. Nowak politely asked me if I would mind sitting down with him while he was having a beer. "It's one of my routines to have a drink before fishing." I told him I didn't mind. As I was waiting for him to finish two beers, he quickly found a "pal" to discuss his passion for hunting.

As soon as we reached the river, Nowak settled himself on a big stone with the attitude of a man who is awaiting great things to happen. He was relaxed and his face expressed great satisfaction as he began throwing the net into the water. After he caught a small fish, he turned to me and must have noticed my displeasure with his "victory."

"You don't seem to like fishing, do you?" the professor asked me with a sly smile.

"I certainly don't."

"Why?"

"To me, torturing animals is no fun."

"Is that so," he said sarcastically. "Don't you eat fish?"

"Yes, I do, and it bothers me when I think about it. But I certainly could never go fishing and have pleasure doing it."

At that moment I came out with something that had been bothering me since my friend Mike and I first visited the professor:

"By the way," I said, "if I had a house, I could never be comfortable having stuffed animal heads hanging on my walls."

"Why not, hunting can be a great pleasure! You should try it sometimes."

"It sickens me. I cannot understand how shooting an animal can be a pleasure. It's bad enough that we eat them... but getting pleasure out of killing them? I can't understand that!"

The professor kept trying but was not successful with his fishing that day. He was getting ready after an hour to pack up his gear.

"Your trouble is you are too soft," he said with a mixture of roughness and affection in his voice. I felt relieved his "fishing party," as he liked to call it, was over. He was ready to go home. Again we passed the Catholic church and the professor crossed himself. I sensed no emotion in him. It seemed as if he did not want to be seen not crossing himself. It felt odd to me, especially since many people passed by without crossing themselves.

The professor stayed longer in Munich than he had expected, so I continued my lessons with him into the winter. One day it snowed heavily on the way to the lesson. Since it was a three-kilometer walk, I needed some time to warm up before I could start playing. He took that "opportunity" to again indulge in nonsensical blabbering about one of his seemingly favorite subjects—Jews. I was not used to being engaged in such talks because the anti-Semites I encountered during the war years were not interested in arguments; they were intent on doing physical harm or, worse, killing. I was also aware that I didn't have the educational background to enter discussions on any subject. But I did know that my experiences had taught me values institutions of higher learning did not seem to offer; a good example was the professor.

Once, as the professor was carrying on with his gibes at Jews and "their financial empire" theory, I asked him jokingly:

"What about Heifetz, Milstein, Elman, Huberman, Rubinstein and so many other Jewish artists all over the world... and the many Jewish scientists, writers and scholars who devote their energies and talents to improve the world and prefer art and science to business? How about them?"

"Stop, stop... Don't be a wise guy! It's silly to mention them. They are exceptions," he said with a smile on his face. I had the feeling that behind the smile lurked a mind that could not be changed through discussion, but I continued:

"What about the Poles or Germans? Are their business people not interested in profit? And how about Mendelssohn and Wieniawski? Did they think of music or of becoming bankers when they wrote their beautiful music, including the violin concertos you like so much?"

The professor seemed startled. Perhaps he was not aware about Wieniawski's ethnic origins, a fact which for anti-Semitic reasons was avoided in Poland. He quickly recovered, and waved me off jokingly.

"Mendelssohn was no more a Jew. His father converted him. Don't you know that?"

"True," I said, "he was baptized, but they did not convert his roots."

"Oh shush, I told you not to be a wise guy!"

Little did I know that these absurd remarks reflected a state of mind that had led the professor to cause a tragedy in the not too distant past.

Professor Novak Keeps in Touch

The time had arrived for Professor Nowak to depart for Frankfurt. He recommended me to a prominent violinist in Munich, Hubert Aumere, an ex-student of Carl Flesh. He held the positions of concertmaster of the city's Opera and Radio Orchestras after the war. I continued my studies with Aumere while Nowak was in Frankfurt giving master classes. I kept progressing while maintaining contact with Professor Nowak. In the summer of 1949, I visited the professor when he came back to Wolfratshausen for vacation.

"What are you up to... how are your studies coming along?" he asked with his usual mix of jocularity and seriousness.

"Remember what I told you before," he admonished me smilingly while waving a warning sign with his finger. "You need to work on technique and studies. To be a good violinist, one has to have not only good brains but also a strong rear to sit on and practice many hours every day!"

"I am finding out now how hard I need to work," I confessed.

"At the moment I am working on the Mendelssohn E minor and Bruch G minor Concertos. I have also done several short Kreisler pieces and Paganini Caprices."

"Good," he said with a pleased smile.

The professor suddenly changed the subject and his face assumed a sad expression: "I really enjoy giving those master-classes in Frankfurt," he confided, "but I must think of the future. I need to live in a country with more musical activity. Life in Germany changed after the war. I must go to America. I would do anything to go there." He knew that our family had applied for immigration to the United States.

"When do you think you and your family might leave for America?"

"Probably in about two or three months."

The professor's face took on a sad expression. He hesitated for a moment.

"Do you think you could ask your family to help me come to the United States when you get settled? I am sure you will not have a problem getting settled. Jews help each other. You will be all right there in no time!"

I was used to the professor's generalizations and paid no more attention to them. The professor's desire to go to the States seemed logical. In those years, it was the dream of many people from war-torn Europe to reach America. But I also had a feeling that perhaps the professor may have other considerations for his urgency to be in America. Why would he feel so strongly about coming to the United States? After all, he was already established and known in Germany.

"I can't promise anything," I said. "It isn't up to me, especially since I would be living with my family. Any decision would depend on their approval. But I'll try my best."

About one year after our family arrived in the States, the following letter arrived from Professor Nowak reminding and urging me to help him come to America:

> *Dear Samuel,*
>
> *I trust that you and your family were able to settle in America without difficulty. I am writing this letter to remind you that I am very interested to come to the States. If you could do something to help me come, I would be forever grateful to you and your family. I will be anxiously awaiting your response.*
>
> *Gratefully yours,*
> *Your teacher.*

I knew how difficult it would be to discuss the matter with my family. As is usually the situation with immigrants, life was very difficult for us. To try bringing a person to the United States seemed completely unreal. Our family was still in the process of trying to find work. I considered myself lucky to have received a complete scholarship at the music college I applied to. There I had to take courses in spite of my poor knowledge of English. I did this while taking on a part-time delivery job for a quilt store on Madison Avenue. I was also aware that my musical background was extremely inadequate, and that I would have to work very hard to earn the school's trust. The fact that I had received the scholarship was nothing short of a miracle since I had to compete with students who, unlike me, had been studying throughout their childhood. In addition, a U.S. government policy requiring job guarantees for immigrants entering the country made the whole issue of bringing the professor impossible.

When I discussed the professor's request with my family, the result was as I had expected. My brother-in-law, Meyer, was upset just at the thought of having the professor in the house. His experiences in Lodz, Poland, were horrific. Members of his family were killed by Polish civilians during the Nazi period. He had long suspected that the professor's residence in Germany during the war "did not sound kosher," as he put it.

"The circumstances surrounding this man don't sound good to me at all," he said. "How could a Polish person wind up living in Germany during the Nazi period without being a Nazi sympathizer? Do you think they admitted him to Germany because of his good looks?"

"You cannot generalize... not all people were murderers," I said. But he was not impressed with my argument. The subject was repeatedly discussed for days, but his position had not changed. Nevertheless, after considerable prodding on my part, my family allowed me to try and find someone who might help the professor come to the United States.

To my brother-in-law's credit, he agreed to even more.

"Let him stay with us," he said, "but you better be right about him. I still think there is something fishy about this man."

To my complete surprise I managed, with the help of an American-born friend, to arrange for the professor's emigration papers. Sergio Rivera was a schoolmate of mine in my first college year. Sergio was a quiet fellow who dreamed of becoming a composer. He also studied the violin, but his talents did not point in the direction of performance. However, he liked to listen to me play. We became friends in the school orchestra. He enjoyed visiting our apartment and would stay sometimes for supper.

On one of his visits to our home, when the letter from the professor arrived, I read it and explained to him the predicament in which the professor found himself.

"Where am I going to get anyone to guarantee work for him? Certainly not with my salary of $13 a week," I complained."

"Assuming he could come, would he have a place to stay?"

"Yes, he would stay in our apartment until he gets settled," I said.

"In that case, I know a friend of mine, a grocery owner, who might be willing to help us."

At first, I thought, Sergio was just having a rich imagination; but it worked.

A year later a telegram arrived from the professor:

> *Arriving by ship... on June 14. Please check time of arrival. Please come to meet me. Your teacher.*

The Professor's Arrival

It was on a clear day in June. Large crowds thronged the pier at the New York harbor. I knew that it would be difficult to find the professor among the throngs of people, but knowing he would be carrying the violin with him, I concentrated my eyes on anyone carrying a violin case in his hands. After about ten minutes of searching, I spotted the professor. He was happy to see me and blurted enthusiastically out a few words:

"Wie gehts, mein Junge, O.K.?"

"Danke, ganz gutt, Herr professor. Welcome to America."

The professor's stay with our family required some adjustments. Although since coming to the United States, I'd gotten used to sleeping again on a normal bed, I did not consider it a sacrifice to sleep on a cot to make room for the professor. The family decided to ignore their own suspicions about the professor, and Mother dutifully cooked meals and tried to make the professor's stay as comfortable as possible.

Professor Nowak seemed quite pleased staying with us. On occasion he even surprised me with views I never heard him express before. Once, on a Sunday early evening our family and the professor sat down for supper. Sergio, my college classmate, who helped arrange the affidavit for the professor, had joined us for supper. Sergio was black, and it apparently surprised the professor that the family felt perfectly comfortable with him. Various subjects were discussed at the table. The professor sat and at times joined the discussion. Suddenly, he turned to me and said spontaneously: "It's really nice to see people from different cultures sit at a table in friendship." He said it with an earnestness and a meditative expression I had not seen in him before. I was quite surprised by that statement. Is it possible that the professor experienced a change of heart and may have had a sense of regret over past attitudes?

After staying with our family for several weeks, the professor began contacting old acquaintances who told him how to get the help he needed to settle down on his own.

"I have good news," he told me with a happy smile one evening after I returned from school.

"I found an organization in Manhattan that helps new Polish arrivals to this country. It looks like they will be able to help me get settled. Would you take me there?"

"Of course!"

The next day we took the subway to the Polish House in downtown Manhattan. It was a relatively small building but there was considerable activity inside. Someone showed us to an office on the main floor. Inside a rather cramped room filled with files behind a modest-looking desk sat a middle-aged, distinguished-looking gentleman. His friendly face, gray hair and his thick eyebrows gave his face a peaceful, grandfatherly appearance. He greeted us politely in Polish. The man introduced himself as Henryk. The professor seemed relieved, realizing that he would be able to communicate with the man in Polish, since his English was limited to not much more than hello and goodbye.

"What is your name, sir?" Henryk asked the professor for registration purposes. His voice was not only polite but kind. The professor obliged. I noticed that the professor left out mentioning his title "Von" when he gave his name to Mr. Henryk and wondered about the reason for his omission. Did he do it out of a sense of modesty, or for some other reason?

Upon hearing the professor's name, Mr. Henryk stopped writing and looked as if he was trying to remember something. There was a moment of silence.

"Your name sounds familiar; don't I know it from somewhere?"

I felt that the way the gentleman asked the question it seemed that he knew the answer already.

"Hmm... Are you by any chance Nowak the acquaintance of ... from Warsaw?" I watched the professor's face; he seemed nervous. It was obvious that something was wrong. Mr. Henryk began trying to make some phone calls. He kept dialing, but apparently without success. There were a few long minutes of dialogue between Mr. Henryk and the professor. The professor was uncomfortable with the talk. He answered curtly and his voice was cracking. It was a very troublesome talk, part of which I could understand.

There were several more questions directed in Polish at the professor. Mr. Henryk got up from his chair, indicating that the interview was over.

While the professor was going to the foyer to put on his coat, Mr. Henryk turned to me, thought for a moment and asked me:

"Could you come over on Monday? I want to talk to you."

After we left the Polish House and took the subway home, the professor stayed quiet throughout the trip home.

I looked at the professor; his face showed sadness and fear. It did not feel right to ask him questions if he did not feel like talking.

After we arrived home and had lunch he told me:

"I have to leave this weekend for Chicago. There is a musical engagement waiting for me there."

I was surprised that he did not tell me that before we went for the interview and accepted what he said. Perhaps, I thought, he did not want to tell me about it in case the engagement might be cancelled.

Professor Nowak stayed with us two more days. During that weekend, I was busy with my studies and helped the professor shop for his trip and took him to the train station.

Mr. Henryk's Information About
Professor Nowak's Student Years

After the professor left New York, I went to see Mr. Henryk. The first thing he asked me was: "How well do you know the professor?"

"He was my violin teacher after the war in Germany and taught me for free. Without him I wouldn't have studied any more. He liked me but I could not help noticing he had anti-Semitic views."

"I am glad you came alone," Mr. Henryk said, "without your family present, because some members in your family might get upset about the things I am going to tell you."

"Thank you. I appreciate your consideration."

"I don't know if Nowak is still staying in your house," Mr. Henryk continued, looking at me intently, "but I consider it my duty to give you more information about his past during the war years in Warsaw.

"Your teacher had a mentor by the name of Mr. Rodin who helped him financially during his studies in Warsaw. I was in Warsaw during the war and got to know Mr. Rodin. In 1939, when the Nazis invaded Poland, and public transportation became off-limits to Jews, Rodin told me that he was planning to visit Nowak to see if he could take him to his parents' house outside the city for a couple of days, so that from there he would be able to escape into the countryside and into the woods and join an anti-Nazi group. I warned Rodin that he was putting himself in great danger just trying to get to Nowak, but Rodin felt that it was worth taking the chance, and that he was sure Nowak would help him. When Rodin returned from his visit, he told me that Nowak assured him he would talk to his parents, and told him to come back the next day. Rodin took another risk the next morning and finally made it to Nowak's apartment house without being caught. When he arrived there, two Nazi soldiers were waiting for him in a corner of the house and arrested him. He was taken to the headquarters, questioned, and later shot. I found out about it from a friend who lived in Nowak's apartment building.

"I feel that you should know about it in case you might have him stay longer in your house. I know you are refugees and can barely take care of your own living expenses, so it is important that you know the facts about this man before you might continue supporting his stay in New York."

I was shocked. In spite of what I knew about the professor's anti-Semitic outlook, I would have never expected him to reach such lows, betraying a good friend in time of great need!

I immediately realized that I could never divulge this story to my family. I did not want to see whatever faith my brother-in-law had left in humanity be completely destroyed.

I told Mr. Henryk that Professor Nowak left for Chicago.

"I am glad for you," he said. We bid each other goodbye. I thanked him for giving me his time, and left with a heavy heart and great disappointment in Professor Nowak.

A Phone Call After a Long Silence

Years later, when I toured with a chamber group we stopped in Chicago. When I settled in my hotel room, I felt a desire to look up the professor in the phone book and find out what happened to him. I found his name and decided to call him.

"Who is it?" a scared voice answered. I recognized Nowak's voice.

"This is Samuel, your student from Germany! Remember me?"

"Ich nothing remember," he answered in a German mix with English.

There was a second of silence.

"Oh, Samuel."

"Yes," I said.

"Feel no good, you hear? Feel no good!"

After he kept mumbling for a while, I realized that Nowak had gone mad.

I recalled our first meeting, Professor Nowak's edginess and feisty demeanor, his strange pride in coarseness and his chain-smoking, his anti-Semitic jokes and his interest in my musical development and in helping me get back to music.

Thinking back, I felt deeply sad that Rodin, his friend, trusted the professor. Perhaps he would have survived if he had not been in contact with Nowak. I also felt angry at myself. How could I have taken Nowak's anti-Semitic comments lightly and not have responded strongly to them? At the same time, I also felt sad for the professor as one does for a human being who was dead for so many years of his life.

On one hand, he helped me and taught me for free. On the other hand, it made me shiver knowing that he willfully caused the death of a good, devoted friend who had helped him realize his life's dream, which he turned into a nightmare.

Sam Marder circa 1980.

A Friend Lost

It is wonderful to live with dreams provided one is awake enough to act on them and make them reality. I didn't think much of that truism until I met Abram.

Abram and I first met in a classroom. It was our first year in college. Neither he nor I had any idea how much in common we had. We sat next to each other and the first thing we discovered was that we could not understand the teacher's psychology lecture. We had both entered college on the basis of our musical potential. The school administration probably took it for granted that we would quickly become comfortable enough with the English language to be able to keep up with the courses.

After a short exchange, I realized that he was also a refugee from postwar Europe and that it was also his first year in the United States. We both had complete scholarships and were studying the violin. We soon became friends. Abram lived temporarily with distant relatives, but felt more comfortable spending time in our apartment, so he visited our family often. We ate meals together, played violin for each other and began seeing each other frequently.

From the first time I heard Abram play, I realized that he had great talent. He had a noble sound. It had a sad quality that carved itself with a strange power into one's soul. He left the listener with the memory of a sound that was unique and haunting. I took it for granted that he would devote himself to his violin studies and become in time a violinist of great importance. But his preoccupations with world matters and his restlessness stood in his way.

After class, we would often sit down over a soda and chat. He unleashed at me his utter dislike of "organized society."

"There is crookedness and injustice wherever you turn. I am disgusted with society. Don't misunderstand me," he said apologetically. "I love people; but when they organize, they become like a pack of wolves—self-centered and more dangerous to each other than wild beasts. Whenever people unite, it is usually against someone and the potential for war grows," he said with frustration. "It always brings trouble. Can't people learn from their mistakes of the past?"

"Being united is not necessarily always for the purpose of attacking others," I argued. "People often feel the need to unite for defensive purposes." He was not happy with that theory.

In spite of his restlessness, he became an avid reader, convinced that he would be able to help save the world with his newly acquired knowledge. His interest in world matters grew. Our talks rarely included personal issues. As soon as we sat down, the world took center stage and, somehow, his music studies stayed in the background. He enjoyed talking about music too. There was even excitement in his voice when we discussed music. But when it came to discussing his own progress, he tried to avoid the subject.

"Did you hear what's going on in the Soviet Union," he stopped me one day on the way to class with great concern in his voice. "Now, Stalin is purging Jewish doctors. It's frightening to know that such a disturbed, sick man is ruling over so many millions of people. And the strange part is that millions are falling for his propaganda and brainwashing."

Abram disliked communism as much as capitalism. "Communism is hiding its ugly dictatorship under banners of propaganda and slogans. Look what Stalin did. He killed off the cream of the communist intelligentsia. Look where Trotsky wound up. And capitalism is hiding behind what appear to be democratic forms of government. Look at how the idea of democracy turned into accepted racism as it exists now in the South. Neither communism nor capitalist democracies serve humanity. Both claim to be for the people and both abuse power and ignore their needs."

His attitude toward religion went through changes from time to time. At first, he claimed to believe in a God that supervises the universe, so he held God responsible for all the awful things that were happening on Earth.

Later, as his English improved, he began reading Voltaire, Diderot, Rousseau and others. "Voltaire was a great man with a sharp mind and cutting tongue," he said with enthusiasm after reading part of his writings. "He was a real fighter for human freedom." But he became shockingly disappointed to discover that Voltaire was an anti-Semite. It was very difficult for him to accept that great minds can have departmentalized brains and are not necessarily as clear in thinking in one area as they might be in another.

His admiration for Rousseau also dwindled when he read about Rousseau's solution to Lisbon's 18th-century earthquake: that people live under the sky, so that buildings will not fall on them. "How a philosopher can have such lack of logic is beyond me," he said with great disappointment.

He highly admired Russell but felt society is not mature enough to accept his ideas. "I don't ever see them coming to fruition," he said sadly.

He never talked about the Bible, perhaps because his father was a Bible and Hebrew teacher. Perhaps he had some reservations about his father's ideas and didn't want to disagree with his dead father. He also never mentioned the Holocaust. Neither did he ever discuss his own experiences during the war. I knew that he came to the States alone, had no parents and survived the Warsaw Ghetto. Beyond that he was only willing to discuss music and the present state of the world.

I later found out that he survived the Ghetto by escaping through tunnels and singing on the streets for food. He would return in the evenings to feed his father, who fell sick. His mother died in the Ghetto as soon as they were taken there.

His features helped him outside the Ghetto. He had blondish hair, blue eyes and a round, Slavic face.

Abram and I were different by nature and background. He was outspoken and projected strength and authority. He was convincing, even when discussing a subject about which he knew little.

I, on the other hand, was painfully shy, introverted and docile. Although at times I was surprised finding within me strength during critical moments, I projected the opposite in daily life.

One day Abram and I left the school together and encountered on the street an alcoholic sitting on the sidewalk talking to himself. Without hesitation, Abram walked over to the man and started a discussion:

"Why do you drink? Aren't you ashamed of yourself, a young fellow like you wasting away your life drinking?"

The fellow looked up at him, surprised. He probably never encountered anyone who would bother to talk to him.

"Do you have a place?"

"Yeah..." the fellow mumbled groggily.

"Then why in hell do you sit on the ground? Are you crazy? I used to sit like you on sidewalks, but I had to. Who is forcing you to act like an imbecile? Go home, shower and find yourself a job and a nice girlfriend, and don't waste your life away!"

Somehow he got the fellow's attention. The fellow, completely surprised at Abram's reprimand, started waking up and began getting up slowly.

"Thanks, brother, you are a good man, " he said, and walked away.

Several days later, I met Abram in school.

"Remember the drunken fellow we met the other day?" he said with a smile of satisfaction on his face.

"Yes," I said. "What about him?"

"Well, he recognized me on the street, and thanked me for talking to him. He told me that he thought about what I said to him, and decided to straighten himself out. How is that?" His face had a happy beam.

He paused for a moment.

"Now I must tell you something private," he said secretively, "but please don't mention it to anyone in school. I found out yesterday that I have tuberculosis and I am being sent to Colorado for treatment. I will be okay. I'll let you know when I get back."

I was shocked. He always looked healthy and strong. We said goodbye to each other. I left sad, but—knowing his strong spirit—hopeful that he would soon recover.

A year passed by without news from Abram. I became worried. There was no one I could contact to inquire about his condition. His relationship with his distant relatives had soured by the time he went to Colorado. After living with them for only a short while, he had moved out and they stopped communicating with each other.

"Why did your relations with your family go bad?" I asked him, after he told me he moved away from his relatives. "After all, they were the ones who brought you over to the States."

"Believe me, there are good reasons for that," was his short answer. He was quiet for a moment and then added:

"They are terribly superficial and I couldn't stand it. I had enough emptiness in my life and don't want to add more to it."

A little more than a year passed by, and I had not heard from him.

One Sunday morning, as I was practicing for my end-of-semester exam, the phone rang.

"Sam, is that you?" I recognized Abram's voice and became anxious.

"Where are you calling from?"

"Where do you think I am calling from? New York, of course. I am fine! The doctors said I can go on normally with my work."

"It's about time," I said with relief. "I missed you."

"I missed you too. Are you going to school tomorrow?"

"Yes," I said.

"So I will see you tomorrow. I want to continue school again."

The next day, we met and I thought he came to rejoin the classes and resume his studies. Instead, he said: "I have a surprise for you; I brought a girl with me. She was the nurse that took care of me in Colorado. We are going to get married this week. You know I don't like fuss. We'll go down to City Hall and get married there."

I was surprised. Why would he get married so soon after his return, especially since he lost so much time? And now he was undertaking additional responsibilities. I congratulated him and hoped for the best. I knew he would have to begin looking for a full-time job and that it would leave him no time for practicing the violin. But that was his decision and all I could do was wish him the best.

Abram did continue his school studies and found an apartment in Manhattan's upper west side. He also found a job that was supposed to enable him to attend school and continue his violin studies.

Abram's wife Lydia was just the opposite of him. She was quiet and did not share in her husband's interests and dreams. She took on a job as a nurse. Abram continued working, but unfortunately only went through the motions of studying. It was obvious that his passion was playing the violin, but he avoided practicing—the only route he had left towards progress. When I asked him why he neglected practicing, he said:

"I can't, I am too restless to practice."

Probably to fill the void he felt from not actively doing his work in music, his apartment became in time a gathering place for hopeful virtuosos. One of his newly acquired friends was Bob, a quiet, intelligent and musically inclined violinist who seemed to have problems with tension that prevented him from functioning with freedom on the violin. Another frequent visitor was Ricky, who was not advanced in his violin studies, but had definite ideas on how the music of Bach, Mozart, Beethoven, Brahms and any other composer should be performed. The discussions went on late into the evenings. Abram enjoyed entertaining them and listening to their playing. The talks were always lively and everyone felt sure he had all the answers.

One evening the discussions became heated. The subject was Bach's unaccompanied Violin Sonatas. A new visitor showed up; his name was Oliver. Oliver was a fellow in his twenties and quite an accomplished violinist. He had already performed in various countries and received good reviews. He played that evening the *Unaccompanied Bach Sonata in G Minor.* Ricky was critical. "This is not the way Bach should be played," he complained. "Bach cannot be played freely; it's not romantic music!"

"I'll tell you a story, maybe it'll change your attitude," Oliver said. "Once Misha Elman came to hear a concert of a great violinist. The violinist was performing the Bach Partita II. When he had finished playing, a lady walked over to Misha Elman remarking; 'That was nice playing, Mr. Elman, but it was not Bach, was it?'

'I would not know, dear lady. I never heard Bach play it,' was Elman's answer."

We had a good laugh. Then he added, "When music is presented convincingly, its interpretation is correct; that's my opinion."

The evening gatherings continued. Lydia kept quiet, showed no interest and did not interfere with the way Abram spent his time. Another year passed and he announced that they were going to have a baby. Abram seemed to have mixed feelings about the idea of a newcomer in the family. He knew that it would add to his responsibilities and make it more difficult for him to follow his passion for the violin.

The baby was born on a cold, snowy day in December and Abram called me to let me know that he took off from work and was on his way to the hospital. I congratulated him and hoped that perhaps the new baby might change his restlessness and give him more reason to work on his music.

The evening gatherings with his music friends continued and I noticed no change in Abram. His attendance in school diminished and he told me that he would have to drop out. "However," he added, "I am not giving up on the violin and will be looking for a new teacher that will inspire me to practice more."

"Neither one of us can afford to wait for a teacher to inspire us," I told him. "We lost a lot of time and you better start practicing on your own, otherwise the best teacher in the world won't be able to help you."

Abram shrugged his shoulders helplessly. "You know me, I'll never make it alone. I feel stuck and need somebody to get me out of this rut."

"I cannot agree with you," I said. "Since the war, I have trouble concentrating. I cannot even concentrate properly and finish a book but I force myself to practice, and after a while I get encouraged to work more when I see progress. Don't wait for anyone to make you practice." As I spoke to him I thought of my teacher Mr. Raff—that's what I shall call him here. "I can recommend you to Mr.Raff," I told Abram, "but don't expect him to make you practice. He was himself one of the greatest talents in Russia but I found out that his teacher refused to continue teaching him because he did not practice. His talent might inspire you musically, but don't expect him to make you do something he failed himself."

I made an appointment with Mr. Raff and went with Abram to see him. Abram did not have much to play for him, but when he played two pages of Corelli's La Folia variations, I could see that he made a strong impression on Mr. Raff. He took him on as a pupil and we both had our weekly lessons on Monday afternoons.

Mr. Raff was a great talent and had a career as a child prodigy. He was destined to become one of the great violinists of our era. He studied, along with the other violin geniuses like Jascha Heifetz, Mischa Elman and Nathan Milstein, in St. Petersburg with the celebrated teacher Leopold Auer, who was very strict with his pupils and only took on geniuses who were willing to work hard. When Mr. Raff showed signs of laziness with his practicing, he let him go. Mr. Raff went on performing for a while, but his great talent could only carry him to a point. Without practicing, he had to eventually give up performing in concerts while still in his young years.

Years later, when I took some coaching from Nathan Milstein, he told me that he knew Mr. Raff when they were small children in short pants, and were studying with Leopold Auer. "I made sure," Mr. Milstein told me, "not to miss coming to Raff's classes. He was quite a talent."

I was amazed that after so many years Milstein still remembered that Raff had his lessons on Wednesdays. Raff's playing as a child must have been very special if the great Milstein did not want to miss them.

Insofar as Mr. Raff's teaching was concerned, both Abram and I found him to be more of a coach than a pedagogue. He would get excited when he was satisfied with our playing. He would accompany us on the piano and offer some musical ideas once in a while. But beyond that, he could not offer specific technical help. When we played well, he would call in his mother and his wife—even one of his neighbor violinists—with excitement and have them listen to us. But in areas where we needed some guidance, he was not helpful.

After a while, Abram began complaining that he did not get the help he needed, although he knew he could not blame Mr. Raff for his lack of practice. Eventually, he left him while I continued studying with Mr. Raff until I graduated from school.

I kept in close touch with Abram. He felt lost and kept looking for a teacher who would offer him help and teach him to discipline himself into rigorous practicing.

Three years passed and his wife kept having babies; a third one was on the way. Abram felt overwhelmed and unable to combine handling a larger family, work, and at the same time continue his studies. He started getting bouts of depression. I tried to recommend him for a job in the American Symphony Orchestra, but it did not work out. He was not used to playing in a group. He gradually began to retreat from his friends and acquaintances.

In the meantime, I was offered a chamber music tour and was away from New York for several months. When I returned, I tried contacting Abram, but he did not answer the phone. I became concerned and decided to go and see him uninvited. When he opened the door, his appearance frightened me. I almost did not recognize him. He had gained a lot of weight and had a long beard. He always used to be clean-shaven. He had a haggard look and his face was swollen. His eyes were red as if he had not slept for many nights. I was shocked, but made a strong effort not to show it on my face. He met me with a cigarette in his hand. I realized there was no point reminding him that he had tuberculosis and must not smoke.

"Hi," I said to him, acting nonchalantly. "How are things?" He didn't answer.

"Can I come in?"

He looked at me as if he was in pain.

"I am sorry. I am not ready to see you. I'll call you as soon as I can," and closed the door.

A few days passed and I called him again, hoping he would respond. This time his wife answered the phone.

"How is Abram doing?" I asked her.

"He doesn't want to see anybody, just stays home. He hasn't been on the street for weeks. I don't know what to do," Lydia said.

"Does he listen to music or read a book?" I asked.

"No, I don't remember when he last read a book or listened to music. He hasn't touched the violin in months. I know he loves the children, but he does not communicate with them or with me either. Several weeks ago," she continued, "we had a visitor from Poland. It was a lady who picked him up from the street after the war and took care of him before he came to the United States. She used to be a singer at the Warsaw Opera. She told me things from his past I didn't know. Once she was on her way home from a rehearsal and she saw this Jewish boy on the street singing. He sounded unusually musical. She inquired into his life. He told her that he lost his parents in the Warsaw Ghetto. She befriended him, took him home and cared for him until he found distant relatives in the States who brought him over. She told me that she found out more about Abram.

"She found a friend of his father who lived next to them in the Ghetto. His father was a Hebrew teacher before the war and when they were taken to the Ghetto, his mother died from hunger soon after.

"Abram found a way to steal away from the Ghetto through underground canals and managed to be able to bring some food back to his father, who became ill and weaker by the day.

"One day Abram came back to the Ghetto and found his father close to death. He had brought back very little food this time. Abram was so starved that he ate up the bread he had brought and did not share it with his father. When he woke up in the morning, he found his father dead."

Lydia's story left me very sad. What pain and guilt he must have suffered after he failed to share the piece of bread with his dying father!

One morning, a week later, I received a phone call from Lydia. She was as placid as I always remembered her:

"I am calling to let you know that Abram died in his sleep during the night. I never saw his face so peaceful..."

Eulogy

It was a nasty, cold January day in New York when I boarded a train for Washington, D.C. The night before, a strong blizzard had dumped on the city several feet of snow. The streets and sidewalks had not been cleaned yet and people struggled in deep snow to get to their destinations.

I got up at six in the morning to make sure the bad weather would not make me late for the train, and was quite relieved to arrive to the station early and board a comfortably warm car. Since I am not a morning person, I looked forward to settling in my seat and hopefully sleeping all the way to my destination. The last wish on my mind was to fill the time with conversation. Within a few minutes, passengers began entering the car and filling seats. I kept hoping the seats opposite mine would not be taken so that I could relax and arrive rested.

Experience has taught me that at the beginning of a trip people usually don't communicate much with each other. They take refuge in a newspaper or book and tend to keep to themselves. But after a while the need for communicating takes over, and if you are lucky, you may wind up with a neighbor who has no need to talk incessantly.

I was, therefore, glad the seats across from mine were empty. It felt good to close my eyes and begin my planned rest. But things didn't go according to plan.

Just before the train began moving, an elderly couple walked into the car, followed by a youngish-looking man, and headed for the seats opposite mine. Well, I thought to myself, perhaps they might also want to rest.

The older gentleman was tall, probably in his seventies, with a thatch of curly, gray hair. His long temples merged with a carefully groomed and waxed Kaiser beard. He carried an attitude of pride on his face. His dark blue three-piece suit, apparently custom-made, fit him to perfection. He certainly gave the impression of a man who was careful about his appearance. The lady, probably in her fifties, elegantly dressed as if she had just been at a party, or perhaps a wedding, was small built, with a thin body. She moved with elegance and youthful flexibility, heading rapidly for one of the three empty seats, while the two men were busy placing their suitcases overhead.

"Are these seats free?" the older gentleman asked. There was an inflection of restlessness in his voice, as if he was afraid of getting a negative answer.

"Yes, sir," I responded with a tired smile that may have appeared to him like a grin. After nonchalantly placing a thick book titled "Abnormal Psychology" on the rack above him, he pulled out a watch attached to a heavy gold or gilded chain from his vest pocket. He checked the time and settled himself on his seat. The younger man took out a magazine from his satchel and held it in his hands impatiently. He moved restlessly with an angry expression on his face, and it seemed as if he was annoyed at the train for not having arrived before it left. There was a short period of silence and I had just closed my eyes, hoping to get some sleep, when the sound of a light cough resonated from a strong bass voice. It was the older gentleman opposite my seat trying to clear his throat. I opened my eyes and noticed him looking me over studiously and with childish curiosity. He glanced at the luggage compartment over me, and seemed anxious to start a conversation. After several back-and-forth glances at me and my luggage, and some additional throat clearing, he pointed a finger at the luggage rack above my seat:

"Excuse my curiosity, but what instrument do you have in that case?"

"A violin," I responded politely but curtly, wanting to get back to resting.

"Oh, a violin..."

He seemed pleased to have found a reason to start a conversation.

"That's a wonderful instrument," he said with boyish enthusiasm. "When I was six years old, my father asked me if I wanted to take violin lessons. I didn't know what to tell him, so he thought it was OK with me and took my silence as a yes. After a few weeks, I got cold feet and refused to continue.

"Do you play the violin professionally?" he wanted to know.

"Yes, I do."

"How nice!" He seemed pleased with my answer.

"By the way, my name is Andy Mazaruder; you can call me Andy, and this is my wife Hilda and my son Desmond." We introduced ourselves. His hand had a powerful grip, and I had to make an effort to straighten out my fingers again.

"Hilda," he said, "enjoys singing in a chorus and Desmond likes rock. I hope that when he reaches my age, he will be able to hear when someone says hello to him."

His voice took on a regretful tone.

"I started taking violin lessons when I was six and decided to stop after a few months. To this day I regret that father consulted with me about taking violin lessons."

"Don't worry, Mister," his wife interrupted. "His father was luckier than he realized. I'm sure his violin teacher must have blessed the day Andy stopped his lessons."

Andy ignored her and raised his voice in frustration.

"My wife thinks that only musically talented children should take music lessons. Music is not only for playing and performing. When children grow up, they should be able to appreciate the beauty of music. That is a great blessing. It certainly doesn't harm to have some kind of knowledge and play an instrument. But the most important part is to get to the point of enjoying its beauty. Of course music is not only for virtuosos; many amateurs enjoy playing an instrument. Look at Einstein. I don't know whether he played the violin well or not, but he passionately loved playing the instrument. As a matter of fact, next to science, music was his other passion."

"But you were not an Einstein," Hilda said laughingly.

"That's just the point I want to make," Andy responded. "Whether you are an Einstein or Feinstein, Eleanor or O'Connor, you can still enjoy the arts! I don't understand why parents ask their children's opinions whether they should study music. They wouldn't seek their advice on whether they should go to school or not, would they? Certainly many children would say no. Children are not mature enough to make decisions about education matters; even when they are older they are often confused about their goals."

He stopped for a moment as if he had to gather his thoughts, and continued.

"Look at our educational priorities in this country. Art has been pushed out of the curriculum in most schools. We disregard the fact that opening our ears to the beauty of music and utilizing our brains toward the discipline of learning an instrument is at least as important—if not more so—than knowing when Henry the Eighth was born."

"Don't you consider history important?" I asked.

"Please don't misunderstand me. I consider history a very important subject. I just don't agree with the way it is taught. Unfortunately, the emphasis is more on dates than on the lessons we can learn from the past."

"The same also applies to literature," Hilda commented. "Children are taught to memorize poems rather than how to understand what they are reading, and some schools teach music the same way. Instead of teaching the students how to appreciate music, they require them to remember when a composer was born and died. That is not the way to communicate the beauty of music."

"Are either one of you in education?" I asked.

"Sort of," Hilda answered. "I am a retired high-school teacher, and my husband was a college teacher in psychology."

"That's more than sort of," I said. "You seem to have spent a lifetime in education."

"I guess so," said Andy. "But now I have many interests. Right now, I am concentrating on the arts. Unfortunately, my experience with the arts in the past was only limited to decorating, a hobby I took up several years ago, and I am thankful that, at least, my eyes are not blind. But now my ears need to be opened up to enjoy the beauty of music written by the great classical composers. At the moment, I am trying to acquaint myself with some of those great works. It's never too late, they say. I am making up for lost time and started going to concerts. I know that, little by little, music will become a more familiar world to me. I have seen it in my friends. Music is like a language, and you have to learn to understand it; don't you think so? And when you do, the rewards are immeasurable. Wasn't it Arnold Bennett who said 'Music is a language which only the soul alone understands, but the soul cannot translate.'"

"Are you going on vacation now?" I asked.

"Oh, no; but I could use one. We are returning from the funeral of a very good friend of mine, and I am very distressed by what I saw. It's an experience that begs to be shared with someone." He reached into his pocket, took out candies and offered me.

Desmond interceded:

"Dad, please don't start again with your complaints. Leave your friend alone. He is dead, let him rest."

Desmond looked in his early twenties. He had a round, shaved head. The clothes he wore were in sharp contrast to those of his parents. He was dressed in black jeans and a blazer and wore heavy boots. He gave the impression of a young man who wanted to prove his independence from his parents. His face expressed frustration and he sat restless in his seat, changing positions constantly.

Andy protested "I am not bothering my friend Raymond. I am merely complaining about his wife and his so-called friends!"

He turned to me: "Have a Life-Saver, it will give you energy." I declined politely. I was hoping to rest rather than hype up my energy with sugar.

"You know," he said to me, "I have a feeling, you, being a musician, would have an ear, so to speak, for what I'd like to say. A musician must be a good listener," he said with conviction.

"Not necessarily," I said. "There are musicians who don't listen well."

"I don't envy you, sir; you will be getting an earful like I did before we got on the train," Hilda warned me.

"Sir, I am afraid I am the wrong person to talk to about funerals," I protested.

"No, no, I know you will understand what I am going to tell you, and you be the judge whether what I am telling you makes sense or not."

Andy cast an inquisitive glance at me to see whether I was being receptive. Having noticed that I paid attention to him, he continued. Seeing that his father had made up his mind to talk about his friend, Desmond opened his magazine with a knowing smile on his face and started reading.

"As I just told you," Andy continued, "I am returning from the funeral of a neighbor down the street from us. We were quite close friends and I knew quite a bit about his life. I am sure he could have lived much longer if he did not have to deal with some of those same people who came to praise and see him off to his final rest. Let me tell you something about him.

"Raymond, my friend, was more than a decent man. Some people are good to their families, but the rest of the world can collapse as far as they are concerned—a sort of primitive, animalistic instinct we all have, if you know what I mean. Such people remind me of wolves whose caring centers only around their own pack.

"Raymond was different. His caring and compassion extended beyond his immediate circle. He was, in his special, gentle way, a powerful, encouraging force in many people's lives. Raymond was a man who embraced a life of simplicity. Even though he was financially successful during his youth because of his great talent in business, he chose a modest life. He worked as a volunteer for a known charity organization. Raymond believed that there was more to life than making money.

"Unfortunately, his wife did not completely share his outlook on life. She felt that in his devotion to his labor of love, he was neglecting their own life."

"Mister, there is more to it," Hilda interrupted her husband. "Would you call someone who has money and likes to live like a pauper normal? Charity begins at home, I say."

She turned to Andy: "Don't underrate Raymond's wife. She did not mind his charity giving, but she felt that they should not sacrifice their lives in the process. She wanted them to live comfortably; and why not? He earned it! Instead, they spent their evenings at home with low electricity bulbs 'because others have less.' Would you call that normal?"

Andy smiled, "That's exactly why I respected him. He was not your average Joe."

Desmond suddenly pulled to the side the paper he was reading. "Mom," he said, "I don't agree with you about Raymond. He was not only nice to strangers but also to his family. The fact that he lived a frugal life to give more to charity doesn't mean he was bad to his family!"

Desmond addressed his father with a touch of bitterness in his voice. "I remember, when I was a child you were impatient with me but showed a lot of patience to others. What would you call that, Dad? You are a psychologist, you should know!"

Andy seemed a little thrown off by his son's statement. "Didn't I give you enough attention, Desmond? Sometimes I thought I gave you too much..."

"Yeah, I guess you must have thought so. Maybe it felt too much for you but too little for me! Remember, I was the child, you were the adult. It was up to you to see how I felt."

Andy had an embarrassed look on his face. He certainly did not consider it in good taste to have personal family problems discussed in public. He tried to find words to answer his son.

"Yeah," he said, "that's the new style. If you are unhappy, blame it all on your father or mother."

"You never heard me blame Mother, did you?"

The mother broke up the conversation. "Let Father tell his story even if I don't agree with his complaints." Andy looked relieved to end the discussion with his son about the past. "My son had been having difficulties growing up, and there is just so much a parent can do for a child.," he confided quietly into my ear. He waited for a few moments to let time dissipate his son's argumentative mood and continued:

"Let me tell you the story and you'll see that my complaints about the funeral are reasonable.

"Upon entering the funeral home, it was not difficult for those who knew my friend Raymond well to imagine how he would have felt had he seen the surroundings. Without doubt, he would have felt embarrassed. The hall projected an atmosphere of pretentiousness with its gaudy, pink carpeting, and its gilded, excessively ornamented chandeliers and large plastic flowers on the podium. In the background, one could hear a young fellow struggling with some cabaret music on an out-of-tune, beaten-up piano. Even to my musically inexperienced ears, the music seemed out of place for such an occasion. Everything was arranged completely opposite to Raymond's spirit and character."

"Dad, why can't you understand," said Desmond, "Raymond's wife was trying to do the best she could to make her husband's funeral as nice as she could. So her taste is not refined. Does that make her bad?"

"No, it does not make her bad. She was only insensitive to the things her husband liked and cared for. There is much more to it. She invited some of his coworkers, who were unfriendly towards him when he was alive. They didn't like him because his devotion and hard work made them feel like freeloaders. They were trying to get away with the least amount of work, and the seriousness with which he approached his work made them feel uncomfortable. They were afraid that his good heart would show their uselessness on their jobs and didn't want him around. You can imagine how all this affected him."

Andy's face took on an annoyed expression. "Could you explain to me what in the world would motivate such people to come and pay their respects to a man they mistreated badly during his life? Did they seek his forgiveness? Did they wish, perhaps, to forget their past behavior towards him? Would you believe that one of these new 'friends' even pushed himself close to the casket to be one of the pall bearers?"

"Is it possible that they felt sorry for their mistreatment of him?" I asked.

My traveling companion disregarded what I said, shook his head in disbelief, and continued. "How did they dare come close to Raymond's casket? How did they dare to show up at the funeral altogether?!"

Gazing intensely at me to see if I shared his feelings, Andy pressed me for an answer. "Am I right, or not? Please tell me if I am wrong."

Having realized that his agitation may have caused his voice to rise excessively, Andy looked around uncomfortably to make sure he did not attract the attention of the other people in the car, but did not notice that two people in back of his seat were listening attentively.

"You have a point there," I answered him with a smile trying to somewhat lighten his excitement. Andy was pleased to have found someone who agreed with him, so he relaxed and was ready to continue, but Hilda seemed annoyed with her husband's excitement.

"How about calming down a little," she told him with a mixture of concern and annoyance in her voice. "If you are not going to stop getting excited, you'll wind up soon at your own funeral."

The tone of voice she used in warning him sounded like it was not the first time he had been warned. She then turned to me. "He is going to make himself sick worrying about how other people behave instead of enjoying his retirement years. We worked hard; it's time for us to get a little fun out of life."

A lady on the seat next to them spoke up. She had the appearance of a society lady who spends her days shuttling between beauty parlors and society parties. She spoke with an Irish accent that suited her green eyes well but not her heavily powdered face.

"Excuse me, but I just could not help overhearing this gentleman's story, about his friend's funeral," she said, referring to Andy. "He is completely right. Any gathering arranged to honor a person, whether dead or alive, should be done with consideration and respect for that person, not with others in mind." Andy had a pleasant grin on his face. He found an additional person agreeing with him. He became calmer and continued.

"Such is human nature—or perhaps education—that some people are prepared to bestow great care and love upon the inanimate world, but are not as ready to give of themselves as much to its living portion. Did you ever observe the concern people show when they get a scratch on their cars? Can you imagine how different the world would be if people reacted with as much emotion seeing a hurt person? What if they treated each other the way they treat their cars? Why it is easier for some people to be nasty with each other than being nice is a mystery to me!"

He stopped for a while and looked around to see whether we were in a smoking car. We were not. He pulled out a pack of cigarettes from his pocket.

"Do you mind if I smoke?" he asked, with a sheepish look in his eyes that revealed a touch of guilt. Having a strong reaction to smoke, I told him:

"Frankly, I think we would all be better off breathing a little more oxygen than smoke." I did it with a smiling face, not to appear rude.

"O.K., no problem," he said.

He slowly returned the cigarettes to his pocket and continued.

"Now, with your permission, I'd like to tell you a little about the service."

"Sure, go ahead." I said.

Having given up the idea of resting, I felt that he might as well be comfortable talking. Andy looked at Hilda and seemed to be pleased that she fell asleep. His son was also napping. He loosened his colorful, red-dotted tie, crossed his legs and continued.

"As services go, it was well organized. Fine eulogies were rendered for Raymond, one surpassing the next in praise of him. How terrible!"

"Why is it terrible?" I asked. "What's wrong with nice eulogies? Don't you like to see a good person being praised?"

"Of course, I do, my friend! That's not my problem. My problem is its timing. It is said—I am no Bible expert, but I think it's written somewhere—that 'there is a time for everything... There is a time for laughing and a time for crying.' Doesn't it say so? In the same spirit it could also be said that there is also a time for praise, too."

"Certainly, there is a time for praise," I said. "But what problem do you find with its timing?"

"Well, we know that the way of the world is to give the dead their due respect. There is hardly a country or culture that does not treat its dead with consideration, care and even awe. And that's how it should be! It's good to see people treat their dead with respect and sensitivity. There was even something positive in the fact that both friend and foe gathered to see this gentle man off to his final rest. Frankly, sitting in the funeral parlor during that hour or so made me feel as if all the negativity towards my friend had come to a sudden halt. It even brought back to me the image of the lion and the lamb sitting side by side in peace and tranquility. I almost dared to ask myself if that is what a glimmer of Messianic times might be like.

"However, as far as I am concerned, it was only an illusion, because when it comes to praise, time and place are very important. Years ago, my good friend, who was now receiving his well-deserved recognition by means of those fine eulogies, had told me how much aggravation he suffered at work from some of his co-workers who now came to his funeral. I also happen to know about the venomous gossip that was used against him."

"Sorry to interrupt," a gentleman sitting next to the lady who had commented on Andy's complaints apologized.

"If it took a strangely arranged funeral to bring together friend and foe, it was still worth it. Look how many living people fail to create peace among themselves. I say, bless his widow! She must have done something right!"

"This is not my point, sir." Andy responded. "What makes me sad is that many people probably never had a chance to know all the marvelous things about my deceased friend until they heard the eulogies. As I was listening to those lovely speeches, it occurred to me that one of the finest qualities we humans can aspire to is the willingness to lift another person's spirit with a nice comment—something that will make him or her feel good. Genuine praise is a wonderful gift. How many people can get along happily without a good word, a nice comment from another fellow human being? No one can live in an emotional vacuum, you know. We are all interdependent on each other."

He leaned over, looked me in the eyes with a sense of urgency trying to see if his idea makes sense to me and asked me abruptly, "Do you agree?"

"Yes, I agree." I replied promptly.

"And yet," he continued, "we all share some guilt at times, in stubbornly practicing stinginess when it comes to being positive with others. Have you noticed that often, when we have something nice to say about someone, we choose to do it in a way that will not reach his or her ear? Praise and positive comments are like a good medicine for the spirit, and probably the body, too. They can have a very wonderful, encouraging effect on a person, provided they hear them. We don't know the condition of a person's hearing abilities once they leave this world. Don't you think it might be nice if people would permit themselves to be kind and say nice things to each other while we are sure their hearing is intact?

"Don't you feel that it would be helpful if people could offer their fellow men and women the recognition and encouragement they so much long for and need during their struggle to survive in a world full of negativity? Wouldn't it be more useful, more beautiful and more rewarding, too, if people could praise their friends and associates, coworkers and students, parents and children, at a time when we can be sure they can hear us, while we can see that gleam of appreciation and gratefulness in their eyes?

"Wouldn't it be wonderful if we could bring ourselves to express as much respect and love for the living as we do for the dead?"

Suddenly, we were interrupted by the conductor: "Tiiiickets, pleeeease, tickets," he droned out his announcement slowly. Andy seemed annoyed at the interruption. He handed his ticket to the conductor without even turning in his direction trying to continue, but the conductor tried to get his attention:

"Sir, your ticket is for Philadelphia. You missed your stop. We are now on our way to Baltimore!"

Andy's face became red and it looked like he was going to explode with anger.

The lady in the back seat who had joined the discussion, hearing that they too missed their Philadelphia stop, looked perplexed and upset. She turned to her gentleman companion who was probably her husband:

"I told you," she admonished him, "that we must not get involved in people's discussions. You always like to do that. Because of you we missed our stop."

The man smiled and did not answer her.

"Why wasn't there an announcement when we arrived to Philadelphia?" Andy burst out in anger. "What kind of outfit is this? Don't you know your stops?"

"I am very sorry, sir," the conductor said politely, "we announced the Philadelphia stop twice, and a number of passengers in this car got off."

"We didn't hear the announcement either," the man and the lady complained.

"You will have to get off at the Baltimore station and take another train back to Philadelphia," the conductor responded calmly. "We should arrive in Baltimore shortly. I will announce the stop." Hilda and her son woke up from their naps and when she realized what had happened, she watched her husband's red face with concern.

"It's not a big deal," she said, "so what if we get home a few hours later? We have no emergencies waiting for us at home. Take it easy and relax!"

"At least you'll have a chance to complete your story," Desmond added with a sardonic smile. Andy, realizing that there was nothing he could do, leaned back and began calming down. Seeing this, Hilda closed her eyes trying to continue her nap while Desmond listened for a while to his father and dozed off.

After Andy recovered, he turned to me, trying to add several things he had on his mind.

"Let me tell you one last thing, my friend. I am not going to wait until I die to have people say something nice about me. No, sir! I am going to arrange a big party on my birthdays and invite all my friends. I want to see the expressions on their faces when I'll encourage them to say some nice things about me while I am still alive, not when I won't be able to hear them.

"I would like to hear good things about myself while I can still appreciate compliments. Why not have the pleasure now while I am still around? Besides, I prefer to have such gatherings while I am still able to invite guests of my own choice. As far as I know, there won't be much chance for me after I die to drive out the people who ignored me during my lifetime. So why not give myself the opportunity to be among real friends and enjoy fully their good thoughts of me?"

The train began to slow down and the conductor droned out his announcement:

"Baaaaaltimore...next stop! Next stop, Baaaaaltimorrre!"

People began reaching for their luggage overhead.

"I wish," Hilda said, "my husband would have paid more attention to his friend when he was ill. I think he feels guilty about it now, and that's why he is talking so much about it. Raymond needed more attention when he was ill."

Andy pretended not to hear what Hilda said. He turned to me and said quietly, "I think she is right. Now I realize that I did not pay enough attention to Raymond when he was ailing.

"Frankly, Desmond also has a point. He is not the greatest son on earth, but neither was I the greatest father. It was nice talking to you. I appreciate your listening. Be well, and the best of luck to you, my friend!"

The trio rushed towards the exit of the car and quickly stepped off the train. I watched Andy through the window and noticed him talking to his son; this time with a more friendly expression on his face.

The Man with the Roses

The bus was inching its way slowly through the rush-hour traffic on Miami's Collins Avenue. My wife and I were glad to get seats as soon as we boarded the bus, knowing the ride was going to be a long one. As we took our seats, I noticed a legless man in a wheelchair. He had strands of palm leaves in his hands. I could not think of a logical reason for him carrying them on the bus. It was not a time of the season when people use them for religious purposes. Therefore, I considered it as just another unexplainable sight one might encounter on public transportation.

The man seemed to be in his forties. His face had a hardened appearance and the deep wrinkles on his face bore witness to a rugged life. But its expression was peaceful, and the look in his eyes made one feel they were smiling and loving. I noticed that he was working with those palm leaves, twisting them elegantly and with masterful speed until he transformed them into a beautiful rose. With his shiny, smiling eyes, he turned to me, gave me one, and instructed me to give it to my wife. He did it with the same expression on his face he had when he was forming the flower. I complied with his wish, took it smilingly from his hands, gave it to my wife and we thanked him.

I looked at the passengers around me. Their faces expressed both amusement and derision. One lady even expressed her annoyance and complained about "the odd people one has to encounter on buses nowadays."

The man continued his work peacefully with the kind of calm that can only spring from an inner spiritual strength. His hands worked with expediency and speed. The passengers on the bus looked on with smirks on their faces.

When another rose was ready, he handed it to a gentleman standing within his reach. The gentleman, surprised, took it smilingly and thanked him. The legless man continued his work, and in about another minute or so had another rose ready. He gave it to a lady who moments before was annoyed by the man's deportment. Her expression suddenly changed when the man handed her the flower with his loving smile. She seemed touched by the man's genuineness and the love flowing from his face, and I could observe in her a sign of discomfort for her previous behavior.

The man continued his work. Since my wife and I sat next to him, I thought it might be a good opportunity to find out something about him because there was, I felt, something unusual about him.

"Where did you learn to make such beautiful roses?" I dared asking him.

He was not surprised at the question.

"Well, it is a long story," he answered me in a soft-spoken tone of voice.

"I know," he said, "you are probably wondering why I do this and why I hand out these roses. Well, you see, I lost my legs in the Afghanistan war and that—believe it or not—changed my outlook on life. Of course my life became more limited after losing my legs. I had to overcome great challenges, but it happened to free me of other, perhaps even more important limitations. It led me to acquire a deeper understanding of life, a kind of understanding I did not have before.

"When I had my legs, I didn't appreciate life; I took everything for granted. Instead of appreciating what I had, I was thinking of the things I did not have, and that turned me into a miserable, unhappy person. I used to wake up in the mornings with a dislike for life and went to sleep at night the same way. The irony was that all the things that made me unhappy and greedy had no real value; I didn't have the slightest understanding how unimportant they were. I didn't even realize how empty I felt inside; I just felt the pain of misery."

He interrupted his talk and looked around. His eyes caught a child sitting two rows behind him, and he asked someone to hand his newly made rose over to the child sitting with his mother. The boy must have been about four or five years old. He took the rose with a childish smile that expressed more than many a grownup thank-you could.

'This may sound crazy," he continued, "but after losing my legs I gained a deeper understanding of the meaning of love and life. They say God works in mysterious ways; He certainly does!

"Of course I am uncomfortable without my legs, but I am happier now than I ever was before. I gained a greater appreciation of life and learned to understand the difference between comfort and inner peace."

While he was talking to me and continued handing out his roses, a strange change of atmosphere began taking place on the bus. Instead of sitting restlessly, looking at their watches and blaming the traffic, the bus driver and God knows who else, the passengers began talking to each other, admiring the man with the roses. It may have been my imagination, but their faces took on a change—a different, more peaceful appearance. It seemed that the legless gentleman was not only an intelligent student but also an effective teacher.

Not every bus ride provides one with an opportunity to learn a lesson worth remembering for a lifetime.

When my wife and I left the bus, I thanked the man again for his rose and bid goodbye to the bus driver. He wished us a "beautiful day," with a grateful expression on his face—not a common happening during rush hour in any city. I left wondering about the meaning of normalcy, comfort and happiness.

PART 3
POEMS

Sunrise

From a dreamy, obscure night
Springs forth a fresh, majestic sight,
A sapphirine early morning regally
Rising from its giant bed,
Changing into its princely cloth
Of velvety, youngish, blushing red,
Stretching wide its golden wings
Over limitless space,
Looking at earth beamingly
With a smiling, bright-eyed face.
Birds ready to begin,
Their early morning prayers
Chirp out in major keys
A symphony of joyous harmonies
From their greenish tint homes
Through chunky, leafy branches
Admiring morning's newborn face,
Singing, dancing merrily,
Praising God's grace.
Bless you, early, joyful morning,
Keep your happy glee sublime,
Nature, it seems, allotted you
A meager portion of its time,
For Creation is in constant change,
A part of God's abstruse design.
It seems you only have hours left,
'Cause soon your sunny, happy beam
Will change into a nebulous,
Silent, nocturnal dream.

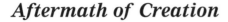

Aftermath of Creation

When God granted birth to Heaven and Earth
And Garden of Eden burst abloom,
Man to dwell there was created, and soon
Truth became mutilated,
Jealousy, cruelty was born with Cain,
And life on Earth was no more the same.

Myriads of years, generations have passed,
Man proudly acclaims his prowess.
With human ego and self-satisfaction
He beats, well pleased, ape-like, his chest.
Impressed with himself he brags
Acclaiming with roars of victory
From his caged-in fences
His giant steps in fantastic advances.

His development gravely neglected,
Life's road remains a perpetual scramble,
When time comes to depart this world,
He leaves it in abominable shambles.
With histories' lessons pitilessly ignored
And failures through centuries blindly repeated,
Observing man's rate of spiritual progress,
Leaves little hope for his happiness.

Lament

A lament
For kindness not appreciated,
For goodness not reciprocated,
Words of praise—belated,
Heartfelt feelings unexpressed,
Warmth in cold silence drowned,
At saintliness frowned.

A lament
For children's dreams crushed by
Hellish years of pain,
For tying up volatile minds
In heavy poisonous chains.
A lament
For hardened hearts unperturbed
By agony of others,
For crocodile tears shed to God
With hands soaked in human blood
Stretched in prayer heavenward,
Praising Creator's omnipotence,
With pride in their human impotence.

A lament
For compassion from hearts erased,
For man looking at brother man,
Not recognizing his very own face.

A Child's Love of God

My early childhood
Love affair with God
A heatfelt love it was,
'Cause a child's love,
The flower of emotion,
Blooms without limitations.
Real, pure, untouched it is,
As the first seed at Creation—
A love devoid of need for explanations.

At age ten, my childhood's soul,
Imbued with miracles of old,
Fed my heart with faith and trust
In God, the loving, kind and just.
But when father's life with millions more
Had been torn away,
Emotions, sharp like steely daggers
Ripped my childhood's heart apart.

Too much human cruelty had
My childhood eyes seen by then,
To harbor expectations high
Of the human race.
Mankind revealed its terrifying fangs,
Its murder-hungry growl,
Watching brother man ablaze.
His blood-tainted claws, too close
Hovered over me in front of my face.
Still, of God's goodness,
With stalwart faith, longingly,
I hoped for a touch of grace,
A small caress I yearned to feel
To soothe my aching, wounded soul.
I searched for God The Merciful
Among the rubble of human grief,
A drop of His Heavenly kindness,
My agony to relieve,
Ease my ceaseless pain.
But for me, a child of ten,
Blurry-eyed from streaming tears,
It felt like a desperate search
Of a broken heart in vain.

Names and Numbers

Names, happenings, incidents, numbers,
Like little children mischievously wander,
Play hide-and-seek inside my brain.
Fresh, unruly, stubborn they became.
Refusing to stay still, they come
And leave at their will.
When fetching them I do succeed,
It fills me with elation,
But when holding on to them I fail,
It leaves me with frustration.
Stubbornly they run about
With impunity tease my mind,
Their games, however, I refuse to play
And will not rest until a way
Their impishness to curb
I shall eventually find.

Remembering Youth

Mysteriously, like an unseen spirit
You removed yourself from me,
And silently, unobtrusively,
On a unknown shore
You abandoned me.
Understandably, you left me
Greener fields to inspire,
New lives to crown with energies
Of freshly kindled youthful fire.
Still, I long for those joyful years
Those times of song and lyre.
I have no qualms, no resentment.
Your mission is a transient one
Dwelling with us passing mortals
During our short-lived journey
On this side of earth's portals.

I take great joy in watching those
Under your gleeful, jubilant reign,
Though, admittedly I must say
It is not the same
Watching you from afar.
But still with closeness
I affectionately greet you
As I do the stars.
And now relegated to
Abide at the edge of that
Never before encountered shore,
My affection for you
Has much deepened,
And increases ever more.

The Matchmaker of Borshchiv

Pesakh the matchmaker, tops in his shtetl,
Had a liking for his trade,
But food on his table from month to month,
Seemed to gradually fade.
Praising singles, so he said,
Is noble, if not always pleasant,
One must like it,
Be ready and willing
To go through life much
Like a starving peasant.

It surely is a special trait
Peculiarities and faults
With a twitch of nose to hide,
Beautify couples in each other's eyes,
Help settle differences,
Good dowries to provide.

However, matchmaking on earth
Seems futile and belated
When heaven ahead of me
Decides who to whom is fated.

Being a matchmaker, he says
Is quite noble and fine,
Much easier, however, is
Selling Challah and wine.

The Village Hupah

She is fifteen, he—sixteen,
Unacquainted, they stand lonely
Under a decorated Hupah,
Encircled by beaming faces.
And bridegroom's parents, sanctimoniously,
Shedding tears of happiness
Drool out excitingly to heaven their praises:
"A bride—a diamond have we found,
Pretty as a fawn,
A beauty like Queen Esther is she,
Ready for the throne.
Her voice—an angel's sound, no less
And the in-laws—no harm in that,
Rich like Korah[1] are they,
Did you see their fancy hats?"
And as people always say:
"From golden carts, a golden nut
With luck could drop our way."
And bride's parents, with sighs
Of Oys and Veys galore,
Drenched with pleasure proudly acclaim:
"His father—such dignified looks
You don't see no more!
The pride of our family
In the village will he be!
And that boy—
No question about that,
A regular genius is he,
A treasure straight from heaven sent,
A miracle from the sky.
Who could ever dare to pass
This brilliant bargain by?"
And the teenage couple
He sixteen—she fifteen,
Lonely, silently, strangers they stand
Under the Hupah and cry

---

1 Bible figure, Levite, who was believed to have been extremely rich. He challenged Moses'
leadership and was punished for his rebellion when fire consumed him and his followers.

Living or Existing

Man rushes breathlessly, thoughtlessly
Pursuing meaningless merriness,
Through a mechanical, robotic life,
With an inflated Me and ignored Thee
He hurries on man-swollen streets,
In cities' teeming beehives—
Chasing imaginary red carpets woven
Out of flimsy treads
of extravagant fantasies.
With telephone at ear, lonely among masses,
Lost in his self-made labyrinths,
He climbs modern Towers of Babel
To drumbeats of dreamed up schemes
What to him alas—an ideal life seems.
Infatuated with illusions of covetous having,
He lives through his years filled
With fantasies of power and grabbing—
A life devoid of sharing, giving,
An existence without living.

The Man with the Bible

He stopped me on the street
With a Bible in his hand
As I rushed for work.
With politeness on his face,
Reading automatically,
With confidence he informed me
Quickly, efficiently and dramatically
That God loves me... but...
I could be saved from burning hell,
If in his church I shall dwell.
Well, so convincing was he
That at the moment I saw myself
At best, turning into a mackerel.

"Do not worry," I said to him
"I do believe God is my friend,
Being good, He could not possibly
Want me burning in fiery hell,
Especially since He loves me.
Besides, a tiny dot I only am,
In God's creation—a little shell,
A pebble in the endless waves
Of God's eternal sea!
Better things than boiling hell
Must God hold for little me.
Besides, hell I have already seen
And felt it well on earth.
Do you think it is my destiny
A dweller again in hell to be?
I do not think, my dear man,
To that God would happily agree."

A Request

Oh you charming clock of mine
I know you don't rule over time,
Still regret your speedy beat,
Your rushing, ringing chime.
Oh, you charming clock of mine,
I know that God rules over time
Only He, the Eternal one is
In its complete command,
Only He decides how time
On earth should run.

My human wish, however is,
If I could only so request:
A modest pause in time to occur,
A stop, of course at God's behest,
That you, my clock, might perhaps
Be granted a kind of Sabbath rest.
It might prolong my earthly aches,
But, would at least, increase my time
For correcting life's mistakes.
How I wish you could be granted
This—my daring, strange request.
But God, it seems, wants only man
Not time to ever rest.

To Ellen Greif

A Way in the Dark

Ant-like man crawls benighted by darkness
Through caverns of his mind,
Burrows, digs with utmost diligence,
A ray of happiness to find.
Yet, his search produces no more
Than what he had before.

Lives with dreams, philosophic mirages,
Claims solutions for world's ills,
Boasts of novel, shrewd discoveries,
Ingeniousness and new skills,
Ignores earth's nature and its laws,
That man reaps only what he sows.
It leads sometime one to wonder
How far from Eden had he wandered?
Some argue he's still in a cave
It is there where he feels safe.
Others say, considering surroundings,
He is creative, industrious,
Sometimes even brave.
But searching only with heartless mind
Certain rays he will not find.
They can be only seen by
Feeling hearts and minds.
For heartless brain and eyes are matter,
And matter without soul is blind.

Autumn

The sky enshrouded in veil of gray,
Listens sadly to autumn winds,
Plucking quivering, snapping twigs
Like aged, dried up fiddle strings.

Wilted flowers modestly bow
To large audiences of grasses
Dressed in wilting yellow
In their season's last performance,
With only winds' applause.

Gloomfully bidding a final goodbye,
The heavy-hearted, dreary sky
Sheds with each raindrop, mournfully,
A tear into eternity, without knowing why.

A Storm

Wild winds hold a frantic dance
On abandoned streets.
Turbulence, darkness, utter gloom
Reign the afternoon.
Out from earth satanic powers
Rip a giant tree,
Like a stick mockingly tossed
Into the fuming, raging sea.

Frightfully, like a mouse I dash
Into a corner of the house,
In fear and trepidation of
The storm's ferocious roar,
A fierceness the like of which
I never encountered before.
With wonder and contemplation
I ponder childishly with a sigh:
What might God be doing now?
Does He laugh or cry?

The Visiting Cat

Mysteriously, the summer evening
Slides into a lazy, peaceful slumber.
From outside the house,
A high-pitched sound, barely audible,
Penetrates the door.
A surprise visitor, I wonder?
Yes, it is an animal on four.
A kitten, black, her nose sprinkled white,
Eyes green and shrewd,
Stands quietly and stares at me
With a curious searching look:
"Hey, two-footer"—winks she,
"Why do you gaze foolishly at me
Through your half-blind human eyes?
I need to eat! Don't you see?"
Into the house I run hurriedly,
Bring a plate of cat delicacies,
Stand and wait wondering,
If eating them she would agree,
But she stands, looks at me:
"Hey, two-footer, do you mind
Showing some courtesy?
I don't approve of being watched,
Cats too need privacy!"

Cautiously the house I enter
In complete retreat.
Silently, I stand and wait.
Open door quietly, carefully,
Wondering whether she ate,
And lo, I find an empty plate.
And from a distance there she stands,
Licks and washes her sprinkled face.
Suddenly, seeing me she stops.
Her eyes, shrewd, greener than ever,
Stare at me with curiosity,
And under her whiskers, freshly groomed,
She throws a cat-like smile at me,
Frisky, fresh and clever.
"Hey two-footer, do you see?
Your language may be strange to me,
Nor do I know your name.
But just the same;
Judge from the platter and you'll see,
My visit was a mighty deal.
I'm not as dumb as you think I am,
And know where to come
For my meal."

To Sonia

Have Seen

Yes, I have seen,
Seen it all,
Good, bad and in between—
Human rise and fall.

Yes, I have seen
When expected least,
Beast in the kind,
Kindness in beast.

Have seen profanity in the holy
Holiness in profane,
Saneness in insanity
Sanity in the insane.

Have seen jealousy, hate
Wrapped in masks of love
Human wolfs in sheepskin dressed
Preaching murder in God's name.

Have seen, beauty in the ugly,
Ugliness in beauty,
A touch of godliness in thievery,
Thievery in so-called godly.

Yes, I have seen.
Seen and felt it all
Ugliness and beauty,
Human rise and fall.

The Violin

Silently waits the violin,
Lonely over the piano.
Quiet but restless, wrapped in silk,
Hoping to be played,
Waiting for caressing fingers
Their strings to vibrate,
Hoping hearts to open
Minds to stimulate,
Sounds and colors to create
Hearts to warm and touch,
Heaven on earth to emulate,
Transcend life into a spiritual state.

Morning in the Andes

I gaze at them, and they at me.
Although a first is our encounter,
No strangers are we.
Sprouting from same earth
We are sort of earthly brothers,
Closer than it seems are we
One to another.

I watch them dip their pointed necks
Into tiny, lazy baby clouds,
Lean my body against one
Of these God-made giants—
These enormous temples of serenity
And feel that peaceful silence
The silence of eternity
Reigning in that motionless world.
In partnership we touch the sky
Under the shy, young morning sun.
No sign or sound of life around,
No trees with birds to help transform
That peaceful morning trance
Into an enthusiastic nature celebration
Of the new day's birth with song,
With joy and playful dance,
With chirping song and fun.

Stoically and mute they stand
These monumental, awkward giants,
They celebrate morning's birth
In their special way—with
Serenity, peace and quiet.
I touch through them the sky above
And realize I cannot fathom
How small I am
In God's infinite order.
With respect, love and awe,
I look at them in speechless wonder:

Yes, you giant, earthly brothers
On that endless stretch of land,
You renew in me a fresh reverence
For God's eternal, powerful hand.

Exit From Paradise

When God created heaven and earth
Earth was completely void.
Darkness reigned everywhere,
And heaven lived in peace together
With the existing earthly matter.

"Let there be light," God commanded,
Planet's surface illuminated
Earth from sky divided,
Water from earth separated,
Fish in waters propagated
And life on earth created.

"All is good," God exclaimed,
And in His Grand Godly manner,
Seemed quite satisfied. However,
One creature still was absent
From earth's paradise
Under the sky,
A mammal walking on two feet—
A creature equipped to lie.

When Adam and Eve on earth appeared,
And dwelt in the Garden of Eden,
Unsatisfied with their lot they were,
Desired to uncover the hidden,
Have a bite from the unknown,
A taste of the forbidden.

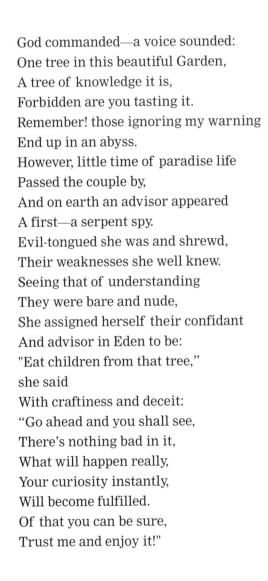

God commanded—a voice sounded:
One tree in this beautiful Garden,
A tree of knowledge it is,
Forbidden are you tasting it.
Remember! those ignoring my warning
End up in an abyss.
However, little time of paradise life
Passed the couple by,
And on earth an advisor appeared
A first—a serpent spy.
Evil-tongued she was and shrewd,
Their weaknesses she well knew.
Seeing that of understanding
They were bare and nude,
She assigned herself their confidant
And advisor in Eden to be:
"Eat children from that tree,"
she said
With craftiness and deceit:
"Go ahead and you shall see,
There's nothing bad in it,
What will happen really,
Your curiosity instantly,
Will become fulfilled.
Of that you can be sure,
Trust me and enjoy it!"

Exit From Paradise., cont.

Having eaten from the tree,
Unhappy they became,
Lost their innocence, discovered nudity,
A new life began for them,
Living a life with shame.
Happiness from innocence
Suddenly vanished, left them,
Embarrassment was born,
Their gained knowledge quickly
Became a prickly thorn.
Missing understanding,
Knowledge led to grief.
Life became a camouflage,
Insufficient was a leaf.
Shame, secrecy and cover-up
Reduced truth to measly drops.
Man's soul suffered damage
And struggles ever since.
Serpentine culture took man over,
Bringing problems strange and new:
Man gained knowledge
And mastered covering up truth.

In Memory of a Friend

Real friendship never fades,
Never dies to memory,
Physical presence not withstanding,
Remains untouched, pure and free.

You were a friend from times of youth,
A friend through aging years.
Our friendship, always present, sailed
On waves of joy and tears.

Your passing on has taught me that friendship
Is spirit that conquers time and space.
Life moves at God's own will,
But friendship never fades.

"Normality"

Feeling normal in a world—insane
Requires a touch of abnormality.
Cure for it—is unavailable
At least in the annals of psychiatry.

Being disturbed by insanity around,
Is indeed a different matter.
A cure for those is offered by means
Of couch and considerable chatter.

Not surprisingly society attempts curing
Those wretched, unfortunate sane,
Allergic to the insanities of
A world's sick brain.

A Blade of Grass

A blessing are you to the world,
An enchanting gift of Mother Nature.
You are one of God's chosen,
To be stepped on and trodden.
Modestly you serve God's will
From the moment of your birth.
Why for that mission
You were chosen,
Is a question lingering still:
Is being trodden so important
To God's plan and will?

Kalman the Genius

Kalman The Genius so he was named
On street, Yeshivah—by one and all.
Young, he was—a boy, a wonder,
Memorized volumes, went into depths
Of Kabbalah, Talmud and yonder,
Problems resolved with inhuman speed.
Town's people with pride acclaimed:
"There's no second Kalman, indeed!"
Year after year on his bench he sat,
With his window tightly closed.
"The world outside," with ire he said,
"Is the devil masked as happiness posed."
Thus, Kalman sat day and night
Deeply lost in heavenly thoughts,
Pushing earthly matters out of his sight.

Once in a while, though, with window open,
His eyes caught glimpses of
A captivating beauty outside,
An endless sky gazing at him
Wrapped in magnificent blue,
Cloud formations peacefully floating,
Grasses glistening in morning's dew
Swaying lazily, in summer's breeze,
And flowers stretching their dainty necks,
Greeting the morning sun.
"But watching them," disappointingly he said,
"Is a dangerous kind of fun.

That will never lead me
Into the world to come."
So he sat, Kalman the genius,
Sat and learned day and night,
Occupied with heavenly secrets
Deeply immersed in otherworldly thought,
Uneasy with the winks at him
From the enchanting outside.

At times, he heard a voice complain:
How do you, Kalman, dare consider
God's creation offensive, hurling it
Like waste out of your heart and brain?
Immediately, however, with lightning speed
A strict voice had him stirred:
Kalman, listen, and listen with care!
You cannot have both worlds here,
Choosing you must only one:
This world, or the world to come!
Beware, My boy, beware!!
Hastily, Kalman turned his head
From the bewitching outside,
And aimed his eyes open and wide
On the peaceful Talmud inside.
"The devil almost captured me,"
He said with regret and fright.
So he sat with window closed,
Learning day and night.
The tempting world still was there,
But no more in his sight.

When Life Is a Show

A curious culture we embrace.
A metamorphosis took place
In our confident, arrogant age.
Life's' rhythm became a repetitious beat
Drummed into ears,
Cool it is to call it "neat."
Its presence cannot be missed
Is felt at work, at home
In bathrooms, elevators
In restaurants while we eat.
Sitting through a quiet moment
Amounts to a gargantuan feat.
From dawn through sunset through the year,
Shrill, loud incessant beats
Deafen, deaden brains and ears,
Desensitize wiggling merry creatures
Blow them out of their seats.
No moment of respite to stop,
Wonder what life is all about.
The beat became the breath of life,
Soul food for all hours, seasons,
Few ever dare to wonder what
Are its underlying reasons.

Ear-splitting sounds beat the pulse of life out
Of dancing, twisting bodies, comatose,
Banging, shrieking out applause,
Without reason or sane cause.

Government, too its partner became
Producing magnificent shows,
Its messages ride on clouds of dreams,
Expecting and getting bows.
Promises are strewn on public arenas
With grandstanding style and entertainment,
Most often followed by public disappointment,
Or worse—criminal arraignment.
News affecting human lives
Joined too the entertainment game—
Reporting value is judged by
Its capability to entertain,
News must not challenge thinking,
Lest it awakens a paralyzed brain.

All in this culture—you and I
Are alas helpful in this maze,
Allowing the perpetuation of
This contagious malaise.
In multitudes we trust and do our best
To help society's gradual regress.
Is there any exit out of this
Negative, cultural mire?
Yes, my friends, perhaps there is:
Create light or experience fire!

Ageless Soul

Observing my soul, ignoring age,
I find it has not ever changed.
Young, fresh and pure it is
Like a heart still in its crib.
Speaking to my heart and brain,
I plead with them and beg: Please,
Learn from the soul facing
Life's challenges and pain.
And like the soul, perhaps
Become young again.

Dog Seminar, Perhaps?

Half a century has passed
And I am still not at my best.
When—oh when—will I be blessed
To come out hiding from my nest.

My dogs train well—their lives not long,
Yet learn their lessons as fast as a song.
A few months training, good food, rest,
And they can be at their best.

When, oh when dear God will we
Be able to achieve our potentiality,
Learn as well as our dogs
In less than half a century?

Freedom

Is there freedom after liberation?
Can Democracy coexist with
Distortion and manipulation?
Is there Democracy without education?
Can truth co-exist with distortion, generalization?
Present and future are holding the answer:
Is mankind breathing health or cancer.
Man craves for freedom from
Power-hungry leaders,
Longs for safety, shelter from
Global disorderly helter-skelter.
Cries for freedom ring throughout
A pained and tortured planet,
But who among its inhabitants
Has tasted freedom yet?
War lives and people die.
People die, and I ask why?

Freedom! Freedom! Free to what?
Free to live in ignorance?
No call loud enough and clear
Is one fortunate to hear:
"Freedom for all man to live
In peace, each according to
His traditions and beliefs.
Freedom to help man see,
That chains of bondage block
His own person to be."

Instead, cries are heard:
"Freedom for me!"
Is it identical with freedom for all?
Freedom from killings, slavery, tyranny?
Some fight for freedom
To exercise abuse,
What value has a tool
Without knowledge of its use.
Alas, so far, nothing positive
Has met man's fate.
The only freedom fastidiously practiced
Is man's mind to manipulate,
Another freedom in high demand
Is the expression and practice
Of bigotry and hate.
That freedom is scrupulously observed,
Generously granted and not interfered with
Until murder is its result,
And stopping it—too late.
Is Democracy automatically
Synonymous with Liberty,
Or in need of ardent defenders
From those who preach it—
Some—its worse offenders.
Freedom for whom, Freedom to what?
That question makes many a heart stop.

Suggested Confessions for Some UN Diplomats

We talk with lofty style two-faced,
We know, of course, it's all a charade.
Of human concern obviously
There is not the slightest trace.
In the halls we kiss, embrace,
Pose for cameras with utmost charm,
Produce cheesy grins,
In that there is no harm.
Fact remains: Theater reigns.
Our mission here frankly is
Presenting tragicomic plays
On world's wobbly,
Vandalized stage.

Speeches at the Divided Nations

Words here, words there,
Wasting hours,
Day in, day out,
Spinning diatribes,
Homilies, praises,
Regurgitating speeches,
Molded phrases,
Fritter away precious decades,
Repeating old slogans
From shining folders.
Any results?
Yes, of course!
Everyone gets older.

Years arrive and disappear;
New dialogues?
Certainly not!
Crafty waves of monologues
Leave world in a rut.
Everyone speaks to himself
With predictable jabber,
Boring tired human ears,
To the point of tears.

Any results?
Yes, of course!
Another generation
On the horizon appears,
Wrapped in old hates,
Plagued by new fears.

Imaginary souls see evolution.
But what, my friends,
Is in a name?
When nothing changes
And all remains the same.

The Loquacious Lady

She looked me over silently,
And soon gave birth
To an hour-long talking orgy.
Why she chose me was quite clear
My plane seat was right next to hers.
With uncanny energy and admirable speed
She unleashed her young life's history,
From early childhood years to
Her most recent love—life victory.
Not untrue to her family,
Each received their due;
Grandparents, parents, cousins, aunts,
Classmates, acquaintances, enemies and friends,
Stories flowed and followed each other
With all respective twists of events.
Fortunately, exhaustion took me over
And politely I fell asleep,
Although not for long, I think.
The young lady woke me up
Announcing our flight's stop.
Thanking me for listening, she said:
"Talking is good for me. It is
My opportunity for a little therapy."
Hesitatingly my head nodded
Reluctantly in agreement,
Wondering what she thought
Was her talk's achievement.

"Yes," she said, as if she guessed
The question on my mind,
"Much I learned from the silence
You just left behind."

On our way out of the plane,
We were met by heavy rain,
She offered me a car ride home,
Declining, I thanked her heartily,
But she refused leaving me
In the rainy dark alone.
Have I also learned something
From this lovely, loquacious lady?
Yes, she left a valuable token
To ponder and remember:
When human hearts are touched,
Neither talk nor silence matter much.

Hope

Think not of a world condemned
Forever to burn in hellish flames of fire.
Or humanity's fate to sink
In floods of tears, suffering and pain.

Somewhere a rainbow is in wait
In the distant skies,
Joyous colors upon earth to disperse,
And dry tears from crying eyes.

Hold It, Please!

Life, I beg you hold back, wait!
So much left unheard, unsaid,
Emotion damaged to be mend
Piles of questions in mystery sealed
So much left to apprehend.
Who wants leaving earth a fool when
Heaven seems to be no school.

With spiritual tears not yet dried
So much hurt left unhealed
Not easy it is in pain to leave.
If leaving time my choice could be
My count would be more leisurely.
A tiny problem, though, exists:
It isn't up to me.

Prayer

Guide me God
To find You
In all of Your creation.

Teach me
To face anger
Without irksomeness,
Enmity with grace.

Help me
Purify my heart from fury,
Edginess with love replace,
May kindness walk along with me
Throughout my earthly days.

Guide me
To escape man's hate,
Its deadly, dangerous claws,
Protect me also from my own
Harmful, negative flaws.

Help me
To see men
As You created them,
Not as they refashion themselves
In countless crippled ways.

Teach me to see life
Pure, clear and bright,
Bless me with a tiny ray
Of truth's eternal light.

Help me God
To free myself
from prejudice
Secretly hidden
From my vision.

Help me,
Protect my soul
From numbness to pain
From near and far apart.
Grant me please
The strength and means
To help those
In need for kindness
From another's human heart.

PART 4
HOLOCAUST POEMS

Shoah

Bodies drift in deadly silence
On a bloodied river Prut,
Faces waxen, eyes glazed,
Staring at a sky in mourning
Wrapped in ashen gray.
The world had no room for them,
Nor soul enough for them to pray.
Trees stand bent as if in pain,
Deadly stillness spreads its dread
Over withering yellow fields,
Its crooked straw-covered sheds.
A crying sound breezes through—
It's a solitary lament
From the barren hill top
The wind wails, moaning.
And in the valley, mounds of books
Engulfed in fire burn without stop,
Swirling, drifting towards heavens,
Searching justice from their God,
Leaving world—page by page,
Hurrying their escape from
Savagery, insane human rage.
Oh God, I cry in desperation,
Daily we acclaim
Your miracles of yore,
Please, there is no time left,
Let your silence be no more!

Translated from Yiddish. Written in Displaced Persons Camp.

A Night on the Way to Transnistria

Casautz[1] was not a forest
For peaceful meditation
On nature's wondrous beauty,
No place for animals
To spend the winter
In tranquil hibernation,
As one might imagine
A forest to be.
It was a place of bestiality
Where earth joined freezing hell,
Where only innocents were punished,
Thousands were gunned down
After beatings and savagery.
It was a place where children's
Pure eyes first witnessed
The lowest of humanity,
Where thousands joined their families
On their final walk to eternity,
Where mothers carried babies dead—
With no time to bury them.

1 *(Casauti in Romanian) a forest in Bessarabia through which we were marched by foot to the Transnistria camps.*

Where sounds of grinding teeth from cold
Mingled with gun shots
Filled the chilly forest night,
A place where bodies, barely alive,
Collapsed on the muddy grounds,
A place where each gunshot added
Another human moribund sound.
Where children's voices' moaning
Echoed through the forest trees
And gunfire was our only light
In the dark of that cursed night.
A place where deadly clamor never ceased,
When only the Heavens were astonishingly quiet.

My Childhood River, Prut

Behold how peaceful runs the Prut!
Its banks and hills—pristine,
No sign left of human blood—
Bestiality was with beauty covered,
Only charm left to be seen.

There is no comment, no prayer
For washed away blood,
For witness left no more
For beauty masking barbarity
On Prut's once blood-stained, cleaned-up shore.

Shoah Memories

Memories of destruction,
Devastation, obliteration,
Are heavy weights to bear.
They live with me, accompany me,
In my heart and mind—
Memories defaced and vandalized
By multitudes of human kind.
Images of children new-born,
Their tiny bodies in halves torn—
Memories of tortured lives
Ending in brutish, cruel deaths.
Bound to their remains I am
As Isaac to the altar.
No angel appears to free me from
The knife of that new sacrifice.
Souls of old and young surround me
In sleep and waking hours,
Cling to me; don't let go
With overwhelming powers.
A heavy burden to bear they are,
There's no shield or comforter,
Sage or seer to lean on.
A half a century had passed
Like clouds drifting by, and
Those memories and I,
Tied to each other we remain,
Through time, an integral part
Of me they became,
A burden I cannot shed.
Must I carry them forever
In a soul torn as the bodies
Of those children—rent?
Must I carry them forever
To the very end?

In Memoriam for Father

You left this world so soon with
My child's heart in unbearable pain,
Eyes overflowing, streaming with tears,
Those marked the final days
Of my childhood years.
In that dark period of insanity's reign
The child in me could not comprehend.
How God, the God of Mercy
Let father's life so young, good and kind,
So quickly and tragically end?
And how you, my father, my teacher
Of life of compassion and love,
Could abandon this world without
Taking me with you
To the heavens above?
Our souls were so intertwined!

Instead you told me not to grieve.
Hours after your tragic passing,
Your emaciated, lifeless body lay
Motionless next to me on the ground.
I listened to your silent heart
Hoping for a breath, a sound.
That silence made me wait
For my last breath
To end the painful wounds.
I fell into a sleep, far too deep
Mother said, to ever wake again.
But suddenly you appeared,
My pain had disappeared.

Surrounded by an unearthly light
You appeared. Your face—agleam
With a euphoric beam.
"Father is alive, Father is alive,"
I shouted with all my strength
In that dream of my dreams.
"Don't be sad, my son," you said,
"Let your heart dismiss the bad.
Don't spend your strength
On sadness, sorrow,
A new life for you is in store
In the not distant morrow."
Your hand touched my quivering lips:
"Here," reassuringly you said:
"Taste this,
A tiny piece of Matzah it is;
It will lighten your wait,
Lessen your fears."
Tasting it, my eyes opened,
Your luminous presence
Suddenly disappeared.
I looked at, saw your lifeless face
Through a curtain of streaming tears,
Waited, hoping for your eyes to open,
But, alas, reality confirmed my fears;
You came to me in dream only
And returned to eternity.

In Memoriam for Father, cont.

But gradually, I discovered
My dream was part reality,
For you never left me, I was not alone.
Your spiritual fountain fills my life
Its treasure is a source of strength,
Although a steep mountain it is to climb,
Difficulties reaching it I don't mind.
Memories of your kindness,
Strength and wisdom
Lift my spirits,
Are lessons for life to learn from.
Forever they will be enshrined
In my heart and mind.

Many years since then passed by,
Your legacy keeps my soul alive;
The spiritual fountain did not dry.
Your image stands in front of me,
Your voice constantly accompanies me,
It did not die.
It vibrates my heart's strings,
Its sound is live and as clear
As in the dream when you appeared
And will accompany me into eternity.

Through hours of despondency,
Sadness, gloom, and fears,
My guiding light you'll always remain
Until our souls unite again
In that forever peaceful world,
A world without tears.

To Eva

*Gravestones commemorate the mass graves of people
(among them the author's father) who perished in Verchovka, Transnistria.*

A more recent photo shows new gravestones in Verchovka.

Transnistria

Transnistria is a region in western Ukraine, between the Bug River in the east, the Dniester in the west, the Black Sea in the south, and a line beyond Mogilev, Belarus, in the north. The designation "Transnistria" is an artificial geographic term, created in World War II. It refers to the part of the Ukraine conquered by German and Romanian forces in the summer of 1941 that Hitler handed to Romania as a reward for its participation in the war against the Soviet Union.

Before the war, this area had a Jewish population of 300,000. Tens of thousands of them were slaughtered by Einsatzgruppe D (an SS mobile squad tasked with carrying out the mass murder of Jews) and by other German and Romanian forces. When Transnistria was occupied, it was used for the concentration of the Jews from Bessarabia, Bukovina and northern Moldavia who were expelled from their homes on the direct order of the Romanian dictator, Ion Antonescu. The deportations began in September 1941, and continued, with some interruptions, until the fall of 1942. Most of the Jews who survived the mass killings carried out in Bessarabia and Bukovina were deported to Transnistria by the end of 1941. According to the records kept by the Romanian gendarmerie and army, more than 118,800 Jews were deported in that first phase. The deportations were resumed in the summer of 1942, with 5,000 Jews, mostly from Chernovtsy, forced across the Dniester River. Also deported to Transnistria, by the hundreds, were political prisoners who were suspected Communist sympathizers. The total number of deportees is believed to have exceeded 150,000. In October 1942, the Romanians called a halt to the deportations to Transnistria, as a result of a change in policy.

The gendarmerie and the Romanian administrative authorities in Transnistria controlled the ghettos and camps. The Jews were confined to ghettos and camps and were all put on forced labor, "for the public good." The winter of 1941-1942 was severe, with tens of thousands of deportees perishing from starvation, the cold, typhus and dysentery.

In March 1944, the Soviet army began the liberation of Transnistria. By then, about 90,000 Jews had perished there.

Source: JewishGen, a non-profit organization affiliated with the Museum of Jewish Heritage, and Zvi Bernhardt.

http://www.jewishgen.org/databases/holocaust/0001_Transnistra.html

Czernowitz

For centuries, this city's name corresponded to the nationality and language of its ruling state. From 1778-1918, the city was a part of the Austro-Hungarian Empire and referred to by its German name, Czernowitz. (Many Jews preferred to use this name through 1944, even as the city's official name changed.) With the breakup of the Austro-Hungarian Monarchy after World War I, the city came under Romanian rule and Czernowitz became Cernauti. In June 1940, the Soviet Union occupied the city. Then in 1941, Nazi Germany attacked the Soviet Union and drove out the Red Army. Romanian troops and Nazi soldiers then occupied Cernauti and massacred the local Jewish population. After World War II, the city once again came under Soviet Union control and it was referred to by the Russian name Cernovtsi. After the Soviet Union dissolved, the city became a part of Ukraine in 1991 and since then has been referred to by the Ukrainian name Chernivtsi.

Source: Jewish Virtual Library (A Division of The American-Israeli Cooperative Enterprise) and Naomi Scheinerman.

http://www.jewishvirtuallibrary.org/jsource/biography/Popovici.html